PRAISE FOR

Listen, Slowly

A *New York Times Book Review* Notable Children's Book

An ALA Notable Book

A *Publishers Weekly* Best Book of the Year

A *Miami Herald* Best Book of the Year

An NPR Best Book of the Year

A *BCCB* Blue Ribbon selection

An ABC Best Book for Young Readers

A Book Links Lasting Connection Book

A Kids' Indie Next List Pick

A Junior Library Guild Selection

"Lại does a superb job of creating a memorable setting and populating it with fully developed, complex characters. Gracefully written, *Listen, Slowly* is a sometimes humorous, always thought-provoking coming-of-age story."

—ALA *Booklist* (starred review)

"The sights, smells, and tastes of Vietnam's cities and villages come alive on the page, without overwhelming a story filled with a summers' worth of touching and hilarious moments, grand adventure, and lazy afternoons."

—*School Library Journal* (starred review)

"As she did in her National Book Award–winning *Inside Out & Back Again*, Lại offers a memorable heroine and cultural journey—ones that are clever near-opposites of those in that book." —*Publishers Weekly* (starred review)

"This is a love story on many levels, between granddaughter and grandmother, grandmother and grandfather, and for the homeland one carries within. Details Lại plants early on add up to a powerful finish. A beautiful counterpart to Thanhhà Lại's *Inside Out & Back Again*." —Shelf Awareness (starred review)

"Lại inserts Ba's lyrical voice selectively into Mai's story. These heart-stopping passages further shift Mai's position from outsider to insider, to, finally, truly bicultural, just as *Listen, Slowly* invites readers to see Vietnam from the inside out—and back again." —*New York Times Book Review*

Listen, Slowly

THANHHÀ LẠI

HARPER
An Imprint of HarperCollins*Publishers*

Listen, Slowly

 For information address HarperCollins Children's Books, a division of HarperCollins Publishers, 195 Broadway, New York, NY 10007.

www.harpercollinschildrens.com

The lines quoted on pages 256 and 258 are from *Vietnam: A Natural History* by Eleanor Jane Sterling, Martha Maud Hurley, and Le Duc Minh.

ISBN 978-0-06-222919-9

Typography by Ellice M. Lee

Map illustration © 2015 by Rodica Prato

16 17 18 19 20 OPM 10 9 8 7 6 5 4 3 2 1

First paperback edition, 2016

For AnAn and her Bà

CHINA
Remote mountain
where Dr. Do-Gooder
Dad disappears
Airport up north
where I see my first
water buffalo
Hanoi, or Hà Nội,
where Út and I find
glowing frogs
Village where I share
the blue goddess room
with Bà
LAOS
South China Sea
VIETNAM
CAMBODIA
The tunnel where
my grandfather was
held as a prisoner
Gulf
of
Thailand
Saigon, or Sài Gòn,
or Ho Chi Minh City
or Thành phố Hồ Chí Minh

CHAPTER 1

I whip my head toward the airplane window as soon as Dad scoots into my row. There's nothing to see except clouds and more clouds, but anything is better than looking at his fakey sorry-to-do-this-to-you face.

Dad is waiting for me to turn toward him. Yeah right. One little glance would encourage another diatribe about connecting with my roots. They're *his* roots, not mine. I'm a Laguna Beach girl who can paddleboard one-legged and live on fish tacos and mango smoothies. My parents should be thanking the Buddha for a daughter like me: a no–lip gloss, no–short shorts twelve-year-old rocking a 4.0 GPA and an SAT-ish vocab who is team leader in track, science, and chess. I should at least be able to spend the summer resting my brain at the beach. Instead, I get shoved on this predawn flight.

My parents slapped me with the news just last night when I was floaty and happy because sixth grade was finally over. I was thinking summer vacation, sunsets, bonfires. But noooo, with buggy eyes and stretchy smiles, they cooed out the news that I "get to" escort Bà, Dad's mom, back to Vietnam for six whole weeks.

"Bà needs you," Dad said when I complained.

Dad goes to Vietnam every summer already, but he'll be too busy hiking toward the most remote mountain to set up a one-man surgical clinic to fix cleft palates and acute burns. I hinted that perhaps he could skip this year but Dr. Do-Gooder shriveled me with facts. Apparently, the kids with hand burns suffer excruciating pain and can't extend their fingers because the skin has shrunk. The ones with holes in the roofs of their mouths live with food and water gushing out their noses. Dr. Do-Gooder always has more demand than he can handle, so at the end of each trip he holds a lottery to pick the next set of patients, who spend a year anticipating his return. Every June, the chosen kids and their extended families travel for days to reach his clinic, forsaking their crops and animals. Surely, I cannot expect him to disappoint them.

Guilt, very big in my family.

Then it was Mom's turn. She too talked about roots and blood then continued ad nauseam about accepting what's embedded inside one's soul, blah blah blah, before letting it drop that, much to her regret, she can't go to Vietnam at all. Something about a trial she's waited three years to prosecute. She's known for always taking on the most brutal crimes against women. Halo, halo.

This is the summer I've been waiting for my whole life. At twelve, I'm finally old enough to take the shuttle to the beach without an adult sticking to me. My best friend Montana and I already got our hair highlighted and bought new swimming suits, hers a bikini with a pink bow smack on her butt, and mine a padded tankini because I have a boy's body. I wouldn't care except Montana thinks not having boobs is like not having hair. She's very proud of hers, but that's like being proud of a sunny day in Southern Cal. As if she did anything to make it happen.

I tried really hard to counterargue with Mom that I too must stay in Laguna; I too must see a project through. But how can I go up against Orange County's golden prosecutor? It didn't help that I had to be vague because I'd die before confessing there's this boy. I can't even think about HIM or I'll explode with anxiety. I noticed HIM as soon as HE went on and on about this poem in class, and after that my stomach flipped like a dryer every time HE was around. HE does have these curls at HIS shoulders, as if that explains anything. I know HE's going to hang at Anita (that's a beach) all summer, and I promised myself I would start a real conversation and actually look at HIM. I have never said HIS name out loud and certainly not to Montana. She has a very bad habit of liking the boys others like first, and those boys have a very bad habit of liking her back.

After I got nowhere with my parents, I screamed and stomped to my room and slammed the door and threw books against the wall.

That last part killed me—I love books. All that drama did nothing.

I'm on a plane.

Dad takes my chin, twists my face toward his and forces eye contact. "I know we're asking a lot of you, but think beyond yourself for just a little while."

I get that my preteen anxieties can't compete with Bà's classic suffering. After all, she lost her husband in THE WAR, which I always think of in all caps. Still, selfish or not, I'm going home as soon as I can maneuver around the sad saga of Bà.

If you think of Bà, you automatically think about Ông, my grandfather. The two always go together, Ông Bà did this, Ông Bà did that. Like saying Mom Dad. Ông was missing in action, so Bà raised seven children on her own. She got them here, pushed them through school, ended up with a doctor, four engineers, a professor, and an accountant. She never asks for anything. Still, my parents and uncles and aunts keep giving her everything. Sweaters, bathrobes, soft house shoes, comfy walking shoes, heater, fan, scented lotion, unscented lotion, big-screen TV because her eyes are failing, back to small-screen TV because the big screen made her dizzy. Endless.

It's hard to believe that Bà would insist on anything, much less on a trip all the way across the world. She has lived with us forever and I've never known her to ask for so much as a glass of water. She hand sews her own clothes, always brown, always cool and soft, washes them in the bathroom sink, dries them in the bathtub, cooks her own rice and tofu and greens, puts them in cute glass containers stacked in the square refrigerator in her sitting room, where she has a tiny toaster oven and a one-cup rice cooker. She rarely leaves her corner of the house.

"Mai, try to understand that this trip is for you too. To see where you're from . . ."

"AAAAHHHHH!" I scream into the airline pillow but immediately throw it down. I'm sure it's infested with lice and stuff.

My scream got to Dad. He's batting his eyes so fast you'd think a bunch of gnats just flew into his eyeballs. Holding in anger, he's squeezing his voice through clenched teeth: "Bà has personal reasons to return home this summer."

"What's so important? All her children and grandchildren are in California. Her life is there. My life is there." I'm loud but don't care.

"Bà has had questions for decades. Be with her as she finally accepts . . . I thought she already did, but that quack calling himself a detective wrote her. I seriously doubt it's possible but . . ."

"What are you talking about? What quack detective? I still don't get why we have to go to Vietnam."

Dad hisses, "Bà thinks Ông might be alive, that's why."

There's no way Ông is alive. I'm being logical here. Bà can be wishy-washy, and Dad can indulge her all he wants, but facts are facts.

Why am I the only one to understand that Ông is gone?

I'm trying to call Dad over to me but, of course, now that I actually want to reason with him, he's at the back of the plane, pressing his index fingers to an elderly passenger's temples to ease nausea. All kinds of people have their hands up waiting for his magical doctoring because they saw him care for Bà after she stirred in the row in front of me. She even got another big blue knockout pill. I asked, but no, I'm meant to endure the longest flight ever fully conscious. BTW, each of us gets a whole row because the plane is so empty. That's how many people are dying to fly to my parents' beloved birth land.

The sooner Dad can convince Bà that Ông is truly gone, the sooner we can whip back to LAX. He should just come out and say it. She's usually the most practical person I know, saving every leftover grain of rice for the backyard birds and brushing her teeth with exactly half a cup of water.

Ông was listed as missing when Dad was two. THE WAR dragged on some more before ending on April 30, 1975. My parents have tattooed that date on my brain. Every year, they still do a ceremony for The Day Saigon Fell. It's been thirty-five years, still . . . solemn faces, solemn faces. I'm shocked they didn't name me April30, instead of Mai (at home) / Mia (at school). Believe me, they are still patting each other on the back for that clever flip. Bicultural, they tell me and beam. I didn't have the heart to tell them I'm uni-cultural. I will, though, as soon as I land back on surf and sand.

Ông has been gone for decades, so long that his youngest child, my dad, now has gray hair. Even if Ông were still alive, and that's a gargantuan *if*, wouldn't he have found Bà by now? As a man of science, Dad will have to concede to the only rational choice left: sending me and Bà home.

Finally, Dad returns. "Why aren't you asleep?"

"Did I get a big blue pill? I don't think so." I can't help that my voice does a sassy singsong.

"Don't talk like a girl with a runaway tongue, you know better."

"All I said was . . . never mind. There's no way Ông is alive."

"Bà is the one who thinks Ông might be alive," Dad says, a bit exasperated. "When I see that quack detective, I'm going to—"

"Gag him with pills?" I can't help but interrupt. I could say so much more, but control. "So the detective has to convince Bà that Ông is gone, right?"

"Right, as soon as she accepts that Ông is truly gone, you both can go home. Mai, I would just like you to be with her until she accepts. All her life this has been her one wish, to be able to accept his passing. What kind of a family would we be if we deny her that?"

OMG, Dr. Do-Gooder just gave me my ultimate wish. I can just kiss life right now. My heart is bouncing so high it might booong out my mouth. I could be at the beach in three days, four at the latest. We will land in Vietnam, Ông will not be there to greet us, we will cry and light some incense, then home home home. I'm trying not to dance. This is a solemn moment.

"It's heartbreaking for Bà," Dad says. "I didn't know my father to miss him and I feel guilty that I don't feel something more. All my life, though, I've tried to imagine what it was like for Bà. They had been promised to each other since he was seven and she was five."

"I've always thought the whole thing was so weird. Was that even legal? What if they grew up and really really didn't like each other?"

"Not those two. Their parents must have predicted how they'd be."

Just then, the rims around his eyes turn pink. For no reason Dad reaches out and hugs me, smooshing my face against his vest with too many pockets. I'm so startled I hug him back, inhaling harsh soap and sour sweat and mediciny medicine. Just as suddenly, he gets up and goes to his row.

I've never thought of this before, but what if Dad went missing? I'd leave for school one day waving bye, to realize later that was the last time I'd ever see him. The idea shocks me so much I sit numb for a long while. I think I would miss him to the point where my insides would disintegrate and leave a charred hole.

CHAPTER 2

Things are looking up. We're at a stopover in Hong Kong, which is fifteen hours ahead so we're already on day two of this supposedly forty-five-day trip. Trust me, I will be trading in my return ticket much sooner than that. Dad, as usual, is off helping someone with something urgent.

Bà waves me over. I go because I cannot displease her, ever. For once, Bà's not wearing soft brown pajama-ish clothes but a tan travel suit, the fabric thick enough for the pant legs not to wobble. Mom bought it years ago and never could get Bà to wear it. Bà rarely leaves the house. She gets sick when a car goes over thirty mph, so she was pretty much sick during every car ride. Yet now she's flying across the world. I'm getting the idea that nothing would have stopped her from going on this trip.

Bà really does have the best smile. Lines spread like outstretched fingers at the corners of her eyes and tiny spears circle her mouth the way I used to draw the sun's rays. The skin on her hands has wrinkles shaped like puzzle pieces, clicking together just so. Her hair is mostly white now, really thin, she's seventy-nine, you know, so the onion at her nape, what she calls her bun, is much smaller than the ones I used to make with her hair before napping with her.

She takes my palm and leaves a quarter of a lemon drop. Always a quarter because a whole one creates too much saliva and cuts the roof of her mouth, while a chopped piece releases just the right amount of sweet and sour. When I used to get put in time-out, Bà would sneak me a quartered drop. It made me giggle so much Mom switched to punishing me with multiplication tables.

"Ăn đi con." She tells me to eat. *"Bà biết mà, không sao đâu."* She understands, no need to worry.

I wish I weren't worrying about what could happen at a little beach back home, but I can no more stop those thoughts than I can talk Dad into putting me and Bà on a return flight right now.

Bà repeats, *"Không sao đâu."* I nod to show her I understand. A lot of Vietnamese still floats around in my brain, though I've never told my parents. It's the one thing I have over them. I know the cable channel code because they kept passing it back and forth in front of me. Not that I am ever left alone to watch anything. And I know all sorts of secrets about my aunts, uncles, and cousins. None at all interesting.

About that clan of relatives, where are they this summer? I

asked, all right. The answer is so typical: everyone is busy. Busy making money, busy doing internships, busy studying for the LSAT, MCAT, GMAT, GRE, SAT. Busy, busy, busy. As the youngest grandchild, I've been ranked most available, meaning least important, meaning the only family member free to accompany Bà.

I used to speak entire paragraphs to her in Vietnamese, so they tell me. But Bà and I haven't really talked since I started kindergarten. On the first day a boy laughed at me when I said, "I see car red." Well, that was a direct translation. I stopped speaking Vietnamese. Bà never learned English.

Still Bà kept talking to me. I would listen and nod and smile really big, like a two-year-old. I wish I could talk to her now. I want to ask her so bad if she truly thinks Ông is alive. I would ask: Who is this detective? Why does he think Ông might be alive? What could he possibly have written to make her fly all the way around the world? When did she hire a detective? Why don't I know anything? I will find a way to ask her. First, we need to be alone and calm, and when time has slowed, we will find a way to understand each other.

Bà hands me an old mint tin. I don't have to open it to know it's full of drops already quartered. I pop another in my mouth. She's right, there's no need for a whole one. Just the right amount of sour sweetness glides down my throat.

I sit still and hold her hand. A fragile hand where the thin skin is almost translucent and each finger bone seems to glow. I don't squeeze but open my palm and cradle hers.

***

The connecting flight seemed to last forever. Finally, the captain announces we'll be landing in thirty minutes and passengers start buzzing. Everyone wakes up, even Bà, and drags bags to the bathroom. While in line, men slick back their hair, and women put on makeup. Soon everyone looks like they're playing dress-up, with the men having changed into suit jackets, and the women into skintight but long-sleeved and high-necklined *áo dàis*, not the most practical travel clothes. The dress, knee-length and split to the waist to create cumbersome back and front panels, is worn with flowy silk pants and high heels.

When the plane touches down, people cheer like they're at a soccer game, some dabbing their eyes. Bà also. I don't feel anything other than embarrassed that I'm landing in wrinkly, sour clothes.

We deplane, pushing an exhausted Bà in a wheelchair down a short corridor, wait in the immigration line and then go to baggage claim. Suddenly, it seems every Vietnamese overseas has landed. I wonder how many have been forced here like me. At customs, maybe because of how frail Bà looks, we are waved right through.

White spots circle my head as soon as we enter the tiny terminal. It's so crowded and noisy I feel sick. Something else is off here. It takes a while to click in that every head has black hair and every face is kinda yellow. Is this yellow-skin thing for real? Mom and Dad always said the three red stripes on the old flag stood for Vietnamese in the North, Central, and South, and the yellow background stood for their united skin. If they were so united, why did they spend years and years fighting? I admit after a long, hot shower the bottoms of my feet do look kinda yellow, but all over, I'm tan, really.

It's freaky to be in a place where *everyone* looks like me. Laguna is 99 percent white, but I am used to seeing other Vietnamese—we eat in Little Saigon all the time. Here though, it's a hundred times more intense. And why does every employee look like they just stepped out of a magazine? All clean and sleek and poised. Girls in *áo dàis*, guys in pencil ties. Every girl is thin and flat chested, the present and future me. No big boobies in this land. Actually, anyone with big boobs would look ridiculous in a demure yet body-hugging *áo dài*, designed for slim frames.

It's an old, crowded, small airport, but orderly. I'd been imagining chaos with screaming babies and stressed-out adults. But I admit most of what I know about Vietnam comes from PBS, especially from this documentary called *The Fall of Saigon*. Mom insisted I watch it so I'd understand—drumroll, please—my roots. The airport in the film was crammed with anxious people camping out with luggage waiting to flee during the final days of THE WAR. My parents and Bà and my aunts and uncles were all in Saigon then, but although I've bugged them plenty I've never heard them talk about what it was like, other than to drown me with the fact that they left to create opportunities for the younger generation. I'm supposed to be teary eyed and grateful, but details, please: How did they leave? What did they eat on the way? Where did they live at first? How did they start over?

Last year, I did a feature on the "Boat People" for the student magazine and had a thousand questions for my parents. Again, I got useless answers like: it was difficult at first, we worked hard, you kids should appreciate the life you have. They finally told me Bà and her children flew out two days before Saigon fell, and Mom left a few years after on a fishing boat. My parents later met at Berkeley. I tried to be relentless but charming in my questioning, like the reporter I might be one day, but Mom looked like she might cry, and she never cries, then Dad shooed me away.

So random roots are encouraged but specific roots are off-limits. Frustrating, my parents.

I'm pushing the luggage cart, and Dad is pushing Bà, who is slumped in her wheelchair. The noise and brightness have wiped her out. Not that I want her to feel sick, but if she's already limpy in her first hour, she's not going to last long here. I do a quick dance.

For every person who arrives, twenty are waiting with flowers, tears, screams. Ông is not here to greet us, as I predicted. I nudge Dad, careful to not sound chirpy. "He's not here."

"He'll meet us tomorrow morning."

My heart stops. "I thought you agreed he's not alive?"

"The detective? Of course he's alive. He's going to convince Bà that Ông is truly gone."

My head pounds. "We're going to meet the quack detective?"

"Let's keep the quack part to ourselves," he whispers. "He started this, so he must end it."

This one quack can clear up everything and get me and Bà sent home. I'm going to be extra nice to him.

***

As soon as we step outside my skin shrivels. The air is on fire. OOWWW! I actually feel like I'm being barbecued alive. Bà has completely drooped. I immediately sweat—it's so strange to be wet and burning all at once. My pores open. My skin turns sticky and oily, like old ketchuped fries. I have to open my mouth to breathe. The PBS documentary showed people sweaty and shiny, but I never imagined they were almost frying.

"Dad, I feel really sick."

"Just humidity. You'll get used to it."

Dad can handle a lot of pain. He bikes up Laguna's big hill without pausing, flies down, then pedals back up and calls it fun. I would have to be rolling on the ground, flames sprouting out my ears, blood shooting out my nostrils for him to give me a modicum of sympathy. I keep gasping like a doomed fish on land. Nope, he does not notice.

A teensy cab comes our way. Bà sits up front because she gets carsick. Dad and I are squeezed in the back with luggage piled on us. At least we have air-conditioning.

Away from the airport, it's green and more green rice paddies. This doesn't seem right. The documentary showed the airport was right in the middle of the city. Bà stirs, reaches inside her bag, and pulls out Tiger Balm, her minty, cure-all ointment for every sickness. She rubs a tiny bit on her temples and holds the whole jar under her nose. Big sniffs. Her other hand twists a knob in the air. Dad agrees, of course. The air conditioner, which makes her even more carsick, goes off. Windows down. Invisible flames whip into the taxi. I feel like one of those desserts Mom blows a torch on.

Even during the Santa Anas, when all of Southern California feels like Texas (says another PBS documentary), Bà still would prefer fresh air because the stale and cold kind gives her a really bad headache. She does allow a fan, pointed away from her. Mom and I either sit around in wet tank tops or go to a hotel. Dad, of course, doesn't even mention it.

I stick my head out. No, it doesn't feel any cooler. Then I can't believe it—right on the roadside, not behind a fence or anything, stands a real, live water buffalo. Chewing on grass, mud on its back, nostrils the size of golf balls, mega croissants for horns. When I was little, Bà taught me a song about a boy sitting happily on the neck of a water buffalo. *Ai nói chăn trâu là khổ, chăn trâu sướng lắm trú, la la la, la la la la.* I never thought I would see one in the wild.

"Stop, Dad, tell him to stop. STOP!"

The driver understands that word for sure. We're thrown forward. He talks too fast for me to understand. That's probably best. Bà groans. I unbuckle and jump out.

"This is so cool!"

Dad closes his eyes, shakes his head. Bà groans some more, sniffing, sniffing Tiger Balm.

It's very difficult to have fun in this family.

CHAPTER 3

I must have fallen asleep, face clinging to the leather seat. Very attractive! My ears actually wake up first to hundreds of *beep, beep, beep*s. We're in the city. Tall buildings, jumbled electrical lines, tons of mopeds weaving between cars and buses. Every single driver is beeping. Who's supposed to get out of the way? There's no room to go anywhere. We inch forward, stop, inch forward, stop. Bà holds a plastic bag in front of her mouth. I might need one too.

There are lanes, but drivers invent their own zigzag ones while squeezing into any tiny opening. One moped goes the wrong way to turn left faster. It's a girl with long, flowing hair. She has a bag with a little dog's head sticking out, barking like it's been kidnapped. Another moped jumps onto the sidewalk, slithers between things spread out for sale: fruit, blankets, coconuts, plastic toys, pots, flags. Wow, a gigantic, dead, pink pig with eyes wide open hunkers down in a cyclo, its driver pushing down hard to pedal. The pig has really long blond lashes. Dad says the driver is rushing the just-killed pig to the open market, where it will get cut up and sold. I'm not sure I want to know this much about where meat comes from.

Even the crisscrossy electrical lines act like the traffic. Just looking up at such a jumbled mess makes everything louder. The smells are in your face too: fishy, flowery, lemony, meaty, grilled corn, fried dough, ripe fruit. Each smell has fists and is smacking each other for more space inside my nostrils.

Yes, this is the Vietnam I've always imagined.

"So, Dad, where's the helicopter tower?"

"What tower?"

"You know, where people pushed and shoved to get out at the end of THE WAR."

"That's in Sài Gòn, we're in Hà Nội."

Dad sounds impatient, but I can't help having questions. "Why aren't we in Saigon?"

"Bà wants to see her village," Dad says, like it's so much work to explain everything. "We'll meet the detective in a hotel here, then it's off to her village."

"Saigon isn't her village?"

"Have you not learned anything about Việt Nam?"

What does Dad think I'm asking about? Russia? There's no reason for him to get uppity. He's been thinking about Vietnam and its many confusing parts way longer than I have. "Where's the gate the Vietcong crashed through?"

"In Sài Gòn, where do you think?" Dad raises his voice. "No one says Việt Cộng up north. Don't say anything about politics at all."

Now he tells me. We're in the North, at a completely different airport, at the hub of the Communists. OMG! "Are they going to arrest us? Do they know Ông moved south and fought for the South?"

Dad really looks at me, as if finally understanding that I really don't know. "Plenty of northerners did that," his voice softening. "Nobody cares now. Just don't talk about it."

As soon as Dad backs down, I don't know why, I get moody. "Fine! Where are the turquoise beaches then? You know, the white sand?"

"We're not tourists." Dad's cranky again. "Stop being annoying, Mai."

Who's annoying?

I wake up to a really loud knock. Dad and Bà, already dressed, should have awakened me. We checked in around noon yesterday and went right to sleep. Now it's morning. That's jet lag for you. We're all in one tiny room in an antiquated hotel because Dad feels guilty living in luxury. Mom is not here to make him. Every seventy-five dollars saved buys one of his patients a bike, so she can whoosh to school instead of walking two hours to and two hours from. I'm all for that, but couldn't Dad at least get a hotel with Wi-Fi? I won't even ask about room service although I'm starving.

No matter, I'm sure the trip is wrapping up. The quack is here. I mean that in the friendliest way.

Dad opens the door while Bà pushes me into a bathroom the size of a closet. I try to get really close to Bà so she can hear my hunger growls and feel sorry for me, but no, in I go. When there's something superserious that adults in my family want to discuss, they always banish the kids. This is old-world child rearing, where it's not required that every family member be made to feel important.

The most I can do is crack the door and peek.

The detective is the most leathery, wrinkly, skinny old man ever. When he steps into the harsh fluorescent light, I can see the bones shaping his eye sockets and jawline. He bows at Bà and smiles, brows wiggling like gray caterpillars doing the salsa. Both say it's been too long, that the years have been kind to them. Really?

While he talks some more, a lot more, I can see yellow teeth blackened at the roots like rotten corn kernels. On him, they somehow look right. I'm hearing Vietnamese but not understanding a thing. I squint, listen harder. Dad keeps trying to interrupt but the detective can't control the hundreds of words gushing from his mouth. Bà is enthralled. I keep squinting, as if that might help me understand.

Finally, the detective takes a breath.

Dad jumps in, his voice urgent, angry even. *"This man let my father go? He was his guard?"* Yeah, I can understand.

More sentences disappear into the air.

"Not acceptable," Bà says. *"Urge him to come to me."*

Blah, blah, blah from the leathery man.

"He last saw my father alive?"

More ghost words. I should have kept learning Vietnamese. But who knew I'd be listening to Bà's most important conversation ever through a cordial yet incomprehensible prune?

"I have money. Is that the problem?" Bà loves to hand out money. She says you might as well spend it when you have it because who knows what man with big dreams will rise up and claim everything that was yours for his cause.

"My mother has crossed the world. This man can certainly get in a van and come to her."

How the wrinkly one can go on and on. Finally, Dad cuts in. *"So it's not money but his* thanh liêm*?"* His what? I've never heard anyone say *thanh liêm*. Dad must be repeating what the detective said. I can't stand people who use five-dollar words. When I use my five-dollar SAT words, it's not like I want to. Mom has branded them on my brain and they pop up automatically. I've been programmed to devour one new SAT word a day, all to satisfy some contest in Mom's mind.

The detective accepts a white envelope from Dad and puts it inside a leather notebook so worn it looks like it might decompose in his hands. He takes out a stump of a pencil and writes super-slowly. As he's going out the door, Dad adds, *"Use every method to bring him to our village."*

Wait, what just happened? I didn't even get to show off my friendly side and the detective left? Did Dad confront him? I come out of exile.

"He told Bà that Ông is truly gone, right?" I put an up beat in my tone because even though Bà doesn't understand English, she's known for guessing the message behind your words.

"The nerve of that quack," Dad says, ignoring me. "He's very good, I'll give him that."

"Ông isn't here, so that means what I think it means?" I repeat, still sounding cheerful.

"Things have gotten much more complicated. Now there's a guard who, of course, Bà insists on meeting." Dad is beyond frustrated. "So you're here until she does."

Gallons of blood flood my heart. It hurts to breathe. I stop being cheerful. Alarm rings out when I ask, "What guard? Did he see Ông alive? When?"

"Exactly!"

"Exactly what?"

No one explains. Dad paces, while Bà sits with her back straight and hand irons her silk blouse. She's worried, and I probably caused half of it. I can't take it anymore, the hunger, the jet lag, the confusion, the guilt. I slam my body on the bed and scream and scream into a pillow.

A hand pats the back of my head. It's Bà. She did this when I was little to get me to sleep. One part of me wants to shout it's her fault I'm stuck in a hot, crowded, sweaty, loud country while another part of me craves her gentle hand on my head.

CHAPTER 4

Dad has dragged me here, and after one little day, he's abandoning us. We're in front of the hotel waiting for our vans. One will take Dad toward some mountain; the other will take me and Bà to her village. Without him, who am I supposed to argue with? Or is it *whom*? Why do I care?

I have a much bigger problem. The guard. Maybe I'm overpanicking. Surely, the detective knows where the guard lives and it's a matter of putting him in a bus or a van. So I should be at the beach in five or six days, tops. I would be so pleasant if other people's needs didn't keep squashing mine.

"I won't learn another SAT word."

"That's your mom's crazy idea, not mine. You'll have your brain filled with Vietnamese anyway."

"I won't learn Vietnamese."

A sigh. "Then be mute."

Ugh. "I'll start making B's."

"If you can stand it, go ahead."

UGH!! "I'll start wearing eyeliner."

"Then get raccoon eyes."

"I'll wear—"

"Listen, Bà has sacrificed everything for us. We've raised you to be considerate, so act like it. Be good, listen to Bà. The detective has to find the guard and that might take two weeks. I should be back before then."

Dad might as well have whammed a boogie board into my gut. "What do you mean 'two weeks'?"

He fake smiles. "It's not that long if you don't obsess over it. I'll meet you in the village."

"Why two weeks?" I hate it when my voice gets all wavy, and this is no time to cry. I've got to plot. For six days I could fake patience, but two weeks? I start chewing off split ends, gnawing at each strand like I'm grinding a steak. How can I be so obnoxious that everyone will be disgusted and toss me back home?

Right then, Dad's cell chimes Mom's ringtone. She must be going crazy, not having gotten us live since we left. Dad answers the phone, cooing, and I'm sure Mom's cooing back. I used to think they were so romantic. What was wrong with me? Finally, Dad tosses me the phone.

"Mai." No one says my name the way my mom does, like she's

packed all the hope in the world into my one syllable. I didn't even know I missed her until now. The tears come and there's nothing I can do about them.

"You're fine," Mom murmurs. "I know you can do this for Bà, and you'll be so proud of yourself. Deep breaths in, now out. From what I understand, the guard is reluctant to come see Bà. It'll all get smoothed out, but that takes time. So hang in there, sweetie. Two weeks aren't that long. Can I hear your voice?"

I can't. My throat is clogged and tears keep gushing.

"You're being so helpful and brave, and try to enjoy your time there because you have no idea what you'll find or whom you'll meet. Be open, love, can you do that for me?"

I wish Mom would stop being so sugary. If she yells and tells me I'm a spoiled baby, I could get sassy. As it is, I just keep crying.

"Listen carefully. Wait until Dad is gone, then look inside the zippered bag that's velcroed inside your luggage. I left you a surprise."

I love surprises. The tears stop even though I don't even want to feel better. It's a cheap trick; Mom knows I can't resist surprises.

"I think you're going to love it. Now before I let you go, your SAT word for the day is one of my favorites. Ephemeral, e-p-h-e . . ."

I jerk the phone an arm's length away, surprised but not really. Mom is Mom. I should have expected her SAT attack. I toss the phone back to Dad.

***

Dad whispers with Bà, then gives her a white envelope just like the one the detective got. Hey, where's mine? I think about not waving bye, but as our van pulls out, I do wave. I miss him already. We talked and Dad agreed that should the detective bring the guard to the village before two weeks, he would return immediately. So I choose to believe it won't be two weeks. Glass half full, that's me. It can't be that difficult to find one guard in a country the size of Florida.

I'm told Bà's village is eighty kilometers from Hanoi. One mile = 1.6 km, so divide 1.6 into 80, where I move the decimal point and make it 16 into 80, where 6 times 5 is 30 and 10 times 5 is 50 so 16 times 5 is 80 and put back the decimal point, so about 50 miles. It's geeky, but I live for conversions. I have no idea how long it takes to go fifty miles here. The traffic in the city crawls along, but maybe once we reach the highway it'll be faster.

It doesn't matter because I'm prepared for a famine. After yesterday, I've made sure I shall never be hungry again. Am I the only twelve-year-old who knows that line? Mom and Bà love Scarlett O'Hara. So do all Vietnamese women, according to this other PBS documentary where a professor talks about how the whole country is obsessed with love, war, suffering, and resilience. How does he know how all Vietnamese feel about anything? Do I count? I'm not so into suffering, war neither.

I've stocked away food that will keep: dried banana sheets, roasted cashews, crunchy mung bean cookies, tamarind balls rolled in raw licorice flakes (I swear they look just like miniature horse poops rolled in hay but taste like sour-sugary dreams), butter biscuits, beef jerky that's somehow fluffy, and, best of all, these crispy coconut cookies that melt in your mouth. When I lost my first tooth and insisted I could no longer chew, I made Dad go to Little Saigon to buy those melty cookies. At times he can be the coolest dad.

I bought everything by signaling for the merchants to write down the cost. Whatever amount each wrote, I counted it out in Vietnamese money. I wouldn't dare bargain. Dad said we are here to be taken advantage of and that's okay with him. Of course, I could only buy food that was cooked, nothing raw or washed in unboiled water. Dad has gone on and on about how my stomach needs time to acclimate to local bacteria, parasites, worms, what have you. And he wonders why I didn't jump up and down to come here? I already had to endure a tetanus shot and a malaria pill as big as my thumb. Sly Dad gave them to me last week and said they were an early flu shot and a digestive enzyme pill. People don't know, but Dr. Do-Gooder can be quite manipulative.

We're passing rice paddy after rice paddy, green rectangles separated by red-dirt lanes. Water buffaloes dot the landscape, rolling in mud, lumbering along dusty paths, so many that I'm beginning to understand they're as exotic as all the stray dogs running around. Once in a while, I see two girls facing each other, holding on to a rope in each hand, and in unison they swing the bucket tied to the ropes. The bucket picks up water from the irrigation pond and dumps it into a paddy. Genius!

Bà has fallen asleep. Another magical blue pill. This way, she doesn't have to endure carsickness.

I lean my head out the window, letting the wind rush deep inside my ear, the sound of a lullaby. It's still sticky hot, making oil ooze all over my T-zone. There's no point in blotting off the shine, more would just come. But I refuse to break out. I will not, I mean it, I will not touch my fingers to my face, which Mom has admonished me against since birth. She works very hard to have minimal wrinkles, even tones, small pores, and, of course, to stay as pale as possible. There was a time, though, when she ran around under the subtropical sun without sunblock, something she still regrets. This part of her childhood she shares once a day. The rest, I have no idea.

I stick my head all the way out, inhaling the scorching air, half expecting my lungs to catch on fire. But they don't. Strange as this sounds, and not that I'm at all getting used to the heat, but any other kind of weather would feel completely wrong here.

The van turns off the major road and right away people swarm us. The driver has no choice but to stop. Bà is awake and takes my hand, knowing I'm a bit freaked out. It's like a carnival outside. People stand five, ten deep, shouting, laughing, crying.

Our passenger door opens and someone lifts Bà into a padded, high-backed wicker chair. I jump out. Our hands have been forced apart, so I cling to her chair as she's carried along. I wish I could tell them to be careful, that Bà gets dizzy easily, but we are smooshed among clumps of bodies.

We stop in front of a tall house painted yellow with red wooden trim. People here really do get into the flag colors of skin and blood. This house towers over all the others. It has five same-sized rectangles stacked on top of each other to create five stories. Each level has doors with balconies facing front and back but there are no windows on the sides.

They set Bà down in the courtyard. She seems overwhelmed. Who wouldn't be? I reclaim her fragile hand and remember not to squeeze. The crowd circles us. Lots of shouts, tears, calls to the heavens, *trời ơi! trời ơi!* Bà starts tiny head bows to no one in particular, so I bow too. The crowd bows back. But no one tries to hug us. Vietnamese do not hug. And definitely do not kiss. They do bow, again and again, plus they offer endless smiles. Bà joins them so I think it's perfectly fine for me to smile too. Suddenly, the whole place hushes. All are pointing at my mouth.

Braces! Sometimes I blank out and forget I have a mouth full of wires. One by one people come up, signaling for me to bend down so they can squeeze my mouth open. Bà nods for me to do so. Not shy, this group. *"Our village has one girl with teeth also covered in wires, our first,"* a man says. *"Now you. Amazing!"*

He speaks normal Vietnamese, so at least I understand him. Only one kid needs braces? Do teeth just naturally grow straighter here? No one around me has braces. But they're older, and to be honest, I see overbites, underbites, crowdings, spaces, crookeds, lots of yellowing. They don't seem to care, so why should I?

When done squeezing my mouth, the same hands reach over

and slap my butt, thighs, arms, head. I'm a one-person tag game. They laugh, finding me highly entertaining. Everyone says *cao quá đi*, so tall. At five feet seven and ninety-eight pounds I slouch even in Laguna, but that doesn't fool anybody. Mom said it's much easier to look elegant when you're tall and have no breasts or hips. That's Mom being comforting. Then someone yanks my hair, saying I have paint on it. Henna highlights. Montana and I were first to get them this summer.

One woman pats me on the head and says she's the third daughter of Bà's maternal cousin whose father introduced Bà's mother to her husband's aunt. What? Bà answers for me and says that I'm so honored to meet her. I do my part and keep smiling.

A man says he's my distant cousin but although he's older he'll address me as Chị, meaning older sister, because my father is a distant uncle to his mother. I smile bigger. Another man says he's the fourth son of Ông's second cousin. This could go on forever because I bet somehow I'm related to every person here.

Bà answers each comment meant for me. Everyone is tut-tutting the fact that I, a Vietnamese, do not speak Vietnamese. Bà has no reply. In my defense, I did not know I would ever need to speak Vietnamese for real. So I do what I can, smile and wave, smile and wave, braces and all. The comments are endless.

She looks just like her dad. Bà answers: *it's a strong bloodline.* Dad and I both have the square jaws of extreme carnivores.

No, much fairer. Bà: *skin like boiled egg whites.* Mom bans me from the sun.

Thin nostrils mean she can keep money. Bà: *that is our hope.* I can store gobs of money and I wish Dad would give me some.

That wavy forehead means she's stubborn. Bà: *as said, the bloodline.* Lots of people have wavy foreheads.

She looks like she knows more than she needs to about boys. Bà wrinkles her brow. Are the villagers clairvoyant? Am I giving off some signal?

Too smart can turn dumb. Hey!

CHAPTER 5

It takes a long while for every villager to have a say, then Bà and her chair are lifted and carried inside where it's a little cooler. I'm right there with her.

The ground floor is one open space storing three shiny mopeds. A garage? On two diagonal beams hangs a hammock, where a boy with a deep tan lies and pets the slimy smooth back of a gigantic frog. Or is that a toad? Whatever it is, it sits on his chest and burps a *ribbit*. Great, I'm in PBS *Nature*.

"Út, put it in the basket, NOW!" That must be his mother hissing because the boy stands up as if every muscle is annoyed, something I do too. No way, it's a girl! She stands there rubbing a military-style buzz cut like she's proud to be one inch from baldness. Strange, but she's kinda pretty, with a perfectly proportioned oval face Bà would

call *mặt trái xoan* and long, thick eyelashes.

The girl rolls her eyes, but the mother doesn't see it. That's also my specialty. She's wearing crumbly khakis rolled up to her knees and a huge, dark blue T-shirt. The girl strokes the frog/toad's head before putting it in the basket. She bows at Bà and stares straight at me. There's no expression. I sneer at her. Can't help it, it's my automatic face. She doesn't even sneer back but looks bored, staring me down even though she's a head shorter. Who is this girl?

We're pushed onto the second level, where food fills a long table. It's definitely hotter up here with air barely moving through the doors facing front and back. What, exactly, is wrong with having windows? Three or four dishes are grouped together under lots of half-moon nets to keep out flies, which are zooming into and bouncing back from the nets.

I recognize cellophane noodles sautéed with bits of chicken and tons of vegetables, dried bamboo-shoot soup with chopped drumsticks, rosy sticky rice with sliced sausages where you can see clear bits of pig fat, stuffed bitter melons, boiled chicken feet, a whole roasted piglet that looks so real it could run away, a gigantic bowl of sautéed leafy greens, carrots and daikons carved into flowers. There's much more I can't name. Everything smells so good.

Long benches run alongside the table. Bà is seated at the head of the table in her cushioned chair. I'm the first one on the bench to her right. Everyone is elbow to elbow, sticky skin to sticky skin. Ewww! Hmmm, if I scream "ewww" and do all sorts of mannerless and embarrassing things, Bà might send me home right now. But

I'm trained to be obedient, I can't help it. One disappointed look from Bà and I would crumple. She's only done it once or twice, and it burned. I will have to force myself to be patient and let the detective do his thing. I've only peeked at him, but I can tell he takes his work way seriously.

The ones who can't fit on the benches hang in the background, offering more helpful comments.

Everyone returns to the water's source.

The daughter of my cousin in Tex-sas . . . she speaks Vietnamese with a crisp northern accent.

My relatives in Cali have a child going to the best college they have, Har-var.

The son of my nephew will be a doctor.

Oh, the comparison game. Mom is an expert. Cousin Justin plays Chopin like a concert pianist, can you? Cousin Brianna won the best science prize in the nation. Can you get a 4.5 like Cousin Dylan? I'm so over it! I'm going to be THE best at something, like pushing back my cuticles. Yay me!

A huge draft goes around the room just before they lift the food nets. All kinds of fans have been switched on to shoo away flies, which try but cannot come in close, buzzing in the background as loudly as my new maybe-relatives. Back there with the flies is hammock girl. She's actually catching flies in a plastic bag! She squeezes the bag in the middle, dividing it into two parts. The top part is a balloon filled with crazed flies, the bottom part is an upside-down bowl, which she inches toward one at rest. As I watch, she traps it every time. Told you I'm in a *Nature* episode.

Someone hands me a bowl of rice, then chopsticks start coming at me and leaving food in my bowl. I don't have time to refuse or accept. My bowl is quickly piled high. Why aren't they turning their chopsticks and using the thicker ends when offering bites to others? That's what we always do at home. Mom forbids spit sharing. A woman sucks on the thin tips of her chopsticks, then grips a chicken foot and jams it on top of my pile. Yuck, yuck, yuck.

Bà quietly lifts the foot away, to where I do not know. She turned her chopsticks. Thank you! See why I always want to please her? She also takes away bits of chicken liver and other unrecognizable parts she knows I've never eaten. She even removes the skin from a chopped drumstick. From now on, she's officially my favorite person on earth.

I pick up my chopsticks and deliver a bamboo shoot to my mouth. Everyone stops eating. Someone says, *"Look, look at her using chopsticks. Just like a Vietnamese girl!"*

What does she think I do at home? Eat rice with my fist?

Someone else asks, *"Are you obedient?"*

It's so annoying when people ask questions with preconceived answers. The man should just come out and say, "I expect you to listen to your parents or you'll shame every ancestor going back four thousand years of Vietnamese history." No pressure. Like any kid is going to admit out loud, "I just pretend to listen."

Food keeps piling up in my bowl no matter how much I eat and eat. I love the smell of sautéed ginger, like a zing in my nostrils.

The buzz-cut girl's mother must know I'm beyond full because she finally waves me over. I stand up and my spot fills in within seconds.

The mother actually takes my hand and puts it in the girl's, saying, *"Go play out back, go on."* We both drop hands immediately. We're not five. Actually, I haven't had to make friends since Montana and I were in Ms. Vollmar's kindergarten class. From then on, all her friends were mine too. So were her enemies. With Montana, I'm guaranteed a great seat at lunch and on field-trip buses. That's worth me controlling my eye rolls when she goes on and on about lip gloss and highlights and especially boys. Thinking of HIM, please, universe, get me home much sooner than two weeks.

"Út, tell her your name, go on," the mother says. Awkward.

I can tell the girl is holding back a huge eye roll. She manages to mumble, "Út," which can only be pronounced by puckering. The most mismatched name ever. Buzz-Cut Girl in no way inspires sending or receiving kisses.

I tell her my name with attitude. "Mia, I mean Mai."

"Her real name is Hương but we all call her Út because she's our youngest. She has an older sister named Lan. They're not alike in one trait. Mothers bear children but the sky gives them temperaments. Lan would never do anything to displease me, but this younger daughter, how she makes my blood flood my brain. Her hair, her skin . . . how I suffer. Now you two go play."

I have no idea if Út's mom knows I can understand. She's just talking to talk, smiling and frowning all at once. She leans over and tries to pat Út's head. Út backs away. I guess parents embarrass their children everywhere in the world.

Út picks up the pet basket and walks off. Her mom pushes me in the back so I'll follow. In the backyard, Út sits with her pet under a pergola-like frame covered with vines of bitter melons. They look oh-so innocent hanging down like tiny, lumpy, green footballs but, trust me, they are called "bitter" for a throat-tightening, tongue-swelling reason. Bà says they contain nature's vitamins. In Laguna, she would stuff and stew them with ground pork, and the whole house would smell green and pure. I've tried to convince her that just smelling is medicinal enough, no need to actually gag it down my throat. But no. Once a month, the bitter bites went down.

Út doesn't even look at me. Fine, I'll just sit as far from her as possible but still get shade from the pergola. With a hint of a breeze, it's a teensy bit less hot under here. I shall never again take the ocean air for granted. In the shade, Út's skin looks even more bronze. Mom would so be running at her with ninety SPF. She packed plenty for me and I've dutifully slathered it on. Mom has drilled me with enough skin cancer photos to make sure I get it.

Út puts her frog/toad on a banana leaf. It's even fatter spread out on the ground. She takes the bag of flies from the basket and unknots the opening, releasing a few at a time. Her pet doesn't move except to unfurl a long, slimy tongue toward dozens of flies, zapping every one. No wonder it's huge.

I'm mesmerized and throw a pebble in the air. It happened before I knew what I was doing. The frog/toad flicks the pebble into its mouth. Then it gags, or what sounds like an amphibious way of gagging. A croaky, pleading sound.

Út snatches it, hangs it upside down from enormous hind legs and shakes, shakes, shakes. The thing throws up. It's not pretty but the pebble does fall out.

"Sorry," I blurt, trying to remember how to say it in Vietnamese. "Sorry, I don't know why I did that." Út glares at me, picks up her pet, and runs off, snatching the basket. Only then do I think of how to say sorry, *"Xin lỗi."*

Út turns around and hisses, exposing wires that cover both rows of teeth.

CHAPTER 6

I thought Vietnam is poor and hot, so to pass time I would be sleeping a lot to escape hunger and the heat. Wrong! Food is constantly jammed down my throat and who can sleep with this many mosquitoes around? Hundreds of them, aiming for me with baby needles, stabbing, stabbing. They're hairy, black, superbuzzy and I swear the size of flies, which are also everywhere but at least they don't sting. Of course, I'm the only one swollen with pink polka dots. Now I know why no one wears capris here! Despite the heat, girls float around in mosquito-proof, loose silk pants and matching blouses. It's an all day, every day pajama-ish party.

We ate for the entire day yesterday, pausing only when the women and girls went to the third floor and took a nap. The higher the floor, the hotter, but that was where the host had rolled out rattan mats on the tile floor. It could have been worse. The men climbed to the fourth floor, that much closer to the tropical sun. Vietnam shuts down in the afternoon because most people get up really early, crash when it's hottest, then rebound by late afternoon.

On my floor, three or four would share a mat and go right to sleep. I lay alone next to Bà's little bed with a foam mattress. I wished so bad I were old. My bones hurt, crushing against tile that I thought was only for stepping on. At least the tiles were cool in the room with no breeze.

I noticed Út was not rolling on a mat. Where did she go? I still need to tell her I really am sorry.

Toward evening, having eaten and napped in the richest, tallest house of all the relatives, Bà and I were allowed to go to Ông's ancestral home. It was a fifteen-minute walk escorted by ALL the relatives, except for Út. They dragged along ALL the food, then stayed and ate and laughed until dusk. That was when the buzzing army came out and zinged my exposed calves, arms, neck, and face.

Bà and I were finally left alone. Well, not exactly alone. I'm learning no one can ever be alone in Vietnam. Ông's younger brother, born in this house, still lives here. He was barely a teenager the last time Bà saw him. She herself was just out of her teens and already a mother. That was in 1954, the year North and South divided, another date that has been tattooed on my brain. Upon seeing each other again, they smiled and held their gazes for a long time, wordless. The weight in their eyes flickered sadness and happiness simultaneously, like in a dramatic movie close-up. Finally, he spoke, telling Bà this house belongs to Ông, thus to her. Bà declined, saying the rightful owner has been keeping it free of cobwebs and mice for a lifetime. They bowed and he retreated to the back bedroom.

I love how polite people are here, but honestly I have no idea if they mean what they say or are just being superagreeable. I think Ông's brother was sincere, but even if he thinks we're back to snatch up his house, he still would be Mr. Nice Guy. That's one thing I get about Út: when grumpy, she shows it, like I would.

Bà and I are sharing the only other bedroom, near the entrance. The room has a full bed with a mattress that actually bounces. The mattress looks brand-new, like Ông's brother got it just for Bà. More than ever, I love being her granddaughter. Last night, we immediately crawled under the mosquito net and Bà fell asleep. I, however, had a mission. The mosquitoes hunted me into the net. Fat and slow from all my blood, they banged against the net trying to escape. So I smooshed them, splattering red all over my palms, flattening black bodies with broken wings. It was so satisfying. Smack, blood. Smack, blood.

We're under the mosquito net again, getting ready for a nap. After being force-fed at breakfast and lunch today, we're tired. I was made to eat so much sticky rice and mung beans, my belly feels like it's packed with bricks. I'm still burping, trying to digest it all.

The net is supposed to be used only at night but I wouldn't let Bà roll ours up. Mosquitoes hunt from dusk to dawn, but I bet there are some who stretch the hours. I feel safer inside the net, lying here and scratching like I have fleas. Bà has already told me scratching only makes it worse. If I ignore the itches, according to her, soon my blood will no longer react to the poison. This mind-over-matter thing has never worked for me.

I've thought about playing up the mosquito angle, maybe scratch myself bloody, moan a lot, shake like I have malaria. That might get me airlifted to Laguna. But doctors back home would run tests and figure out I faked the whole thing and Mom would ship me right back, probably for the entire summer. So I've got to suck it up and wait for the detective to bring the guard. Then Bà can ask all her questions. Tears. Acceptance. Incense. Home. Not much else can happen.

Bà pulls out her Tiger Balm. Bad, bad sign. How could I have forgotten about her cure-all weapon? I stop scratching and forbid myself to touch even one pink bump, but it's too late. Bà is twisting open the shiny metal lid and reaching out for me. Why did I have to call attention to myself? She holds up my right arm and meticulously rubs the ointment on each pink dot. You know what a minty, burning, menthol-y goo does to mosquito bites? It makes them itch even more! But I can't reason with Bà about Tiger Balm, which she has anointed with the power to blast away headaches, backaches, joint aches, stomachaches, nausea, seasickness, carsickness, burns, bites, gas, congestion . . . just to name a few.

Now Bà wants my other arm. Noooo. I quickly stick my finger into the jar, scoop out a pungent glob and pretend to rub it on my bites. I'm actually massaging it on the flat skin surrounding the bumps. Even so, it burns. Bà waits for me to assault my calves and ankles and feet and neck and face. My eyes have turned into waterfalls. Tiger Balm is no joke. Finally, Bà closes the lid.

"Guess what once floated on that wall?" Bà asks. I always understand whatever Bà says because she uses only the words she has taught me.

Through stinging eyes, I kinda see that on the wall used to be a mural, made of blue tiles. Most have fallen off, leaving pockmarks on the dingy wall. Everything in the house is cracked and gray. Outside, the year *1929* is carved into the wood above the doorway. Bà said Ông was born that year and, to celebrate, his father designed a house inspired by his travels: one story, tile roof, brick walls, windows facing every direction, rooms that extend out instead of up, and a garden that claimed much more land than the house itself.

I suddenly remember the word for blue, *"Xanh."*

"Yes. Remember our stories about the goddess in a blue robe that drifts like tea vapors? Remnants of her gown still remain."

I do remember, smiling big to show Bà. Twice a day I used to hear long stories, one at nap time and one before bed. Then I went to kindergarten and stopped listening.

"I have known Ông since the beginning of memories, matched as one from his seventh year, my fifth. Marriage to be delayed until he had studied in France, I in Japan. Yet war reached us. We were joined at eighteen, sixteen. Too soon. The day of our wedding a snake line of

people arrived at our door. They bore drums and flags and silver gift trays covered in red velvet. The first two days proved simple to hide from him, so many relatives, so many ceremonies. But the third day, four men with muscles like twisted laundry carried me in a palanquin to his parents' door. As taught, I took steps light as a crane's into the house, bowed before the ancestral altar. While everyone prayed, I retreated inside the first room with a door.

"This one. The bridal chamber. In pink silk a bed floated, from above a blue goddess gazed. I pushed an armoire against the door and sat on the floor counting the thumps from my heart. Out there they pleaded, then threatened, then my father thundered. Yet, I sat. The season was spring. Peach petals drifted outside the open window. I jumped up. Too late. Ông was perched on the windowsill, having climbed the peach tree. I pushed him back and slammed the bamboo shutters. His shape showed through, even the hint of curls by his ears. His voice seeped through too. Ah, that voice. In such a voice, sharp tones shattered and landed in drops of bells. He talked until the sun shriveled to an orange-yellow seed. He talked until I released the shutters.

"For years now, I've counted the hours I had lost, that day and days after, when I was reading or visiting relatives or daydreaming, hours I could have been beside him. For years, I've counted the hours ever after as I wait for some part of him to return to me. I'm no dreamer. Raising seven children during war has a way of slapping reality into one's fate. And yet, against reason, I continue to wait."

"Ông sống?" Ông alive? I suck in a huge breath, willing this to

be the right moment to ask. I softly squeeze Bà's hand to mean I've been thinking about this for some time.

Bà understands; she always has. I don't know how, but Bà has always known how I feel at any given moment, especially when I'm sad, especially when I'm in need of a quartered lemon drop.

"I do not live on butterfly wings, my child. His chances of remaining among us rank as likely as finding an ebony orchid. Yet I hold on to hope because I have been unable to imagine his ending. If intact, he would have returned to this room. We promised should life separate us, we would rejoin under the blue goddess. He never returned to us, but he never truly departed. I came here knowing I will unlikely be granted him in person, but perhaps I will be allowed to reclaim something of his, anything at all. The guard knows how Ông spent his days, what he ate, what he wore, what he said, the weight in his eyes, the shade of his skin, the whistle of his breaths. I need to absorb every morsel deemed knowable, then I have vowed to release the heaviness of longing."

Bà lets go of my hand and turns from me. Time to let her rest.

My body loosens and expands, remembering how it used to make room for her words to wiggle deep into the tiny crevices alongside my bones, muscles, and joints. Becoming a part of me. I've always been able to imagine her as a rich girl who grew up in wartime and ended up raising seven children alone. She always says, *"Cờ đến tay, phải phất."* Flag in hand, you must wave it. It wasn't about being brave or extraordinary so much as inhaling all the way to her core and accepting her responsibilities.

But I have never understood how she got through her loss. How do you know someone almost since birth, then one day you know absolutely nothing more about him at all? Ông Bà made plans, she told me, plans of how to educate their children, how to care for their parents, how to wait for peace, how to behave in old age. They did not plan on being apart after he was thirty-seven and she thirty-five. I used to think that was old, but that was much younger than Mom and Dad now.

Bà has fallen asleep. Her snores will deepen. I roll toward her and inhale Tiger Balm mixed with BenGay, all the way down to my toes. The most tingly, comforting scent there is.

CHAPTER 7

I hear whistling—the kind humans make when trying to sound like a bird. I crawl out of the net, then jiggle to make it hard for rebellious, day-hunter mosquitoes to stab my exposed skin. Mom packed for me, all capris, as I was too busy seething. I can just hear her reasoning: skirts too impractical, shorts too revealing, pants too hot, so let's do capris. Mosquitoes all over Vietnam cheered.

Thinking of Mom, I run to my luggage, yank free the velcroed pocket, and unzip it to find a palm-sized something inside bubble wrap. Rip . . . revealing a cell phone and a charger. I take a deep breath and stare. This must be what it felt like to find gold. I actually kiss the cell. I should have known Mom would find a way to circumvent Dad's ban on anything electronic, as not to show off. But I need this. Why did I not find it immediately after talking to Mom yesterday morning? Because life in Vietnam is one body-crushing, must-do, crowd-throbbing, mind-heavy event after another. It takes all my energy just to react.

I zoom around trying to find an outlet. Nothing. Can life be this cruel? Control, I tell myself, control. I will find a way to charge the phone, then I'm practically back in Laguna.

I run outside and stop short. A pouting Út stands in the courtyard in yesterday's crumpled pants and T-shirt. Three teenagers, all clutching sun-blocking umbrellas, surround her as if she might run off. I bet they had to pull her toward me the whole way. They wave, a skinny boy and two long-haired girls, all wearing long pants in this sticky heat. Of course they're not scratching or jiggling. Út is, surprise surprise, cradling her pet. The others each hold a basket.

With his umbrella hand, the boy reaches out for one of the older girls' baskets. She's got to be Út's sister, Lan. The same perfect oval face, same movie-star eyelashes, but Lan seems prettier because, let's face it, a buzz cut takes down even the best of us. The boy looks straight at Lan and smiles, not just smiles, but beams the universal signal for "Interested." She looks down, turns really pink, smiles at the ground. Even I'm not that bad in front of HIM. I catch her smile just in time to see a slight overbite.

Before Lan can give him her basket, the other girl jams her basket into his hand. The universal gesture for "You Better Not Be Interested in Her!" This girl looks right at him and wiggles her hips. She actually does that, bold and mocking—such a Montana-ish move. The boy swallows; the knot at his throat runs up and down.

He decides to carry the umbrella and one basket on the left, and the other two baskets on the right. Poor guy, I can tell this triangle is nowhere near over.

The boy steps forward. "Good aft'noon, miss. My name is Minh. I would be honored to serve as your translator if you can forgive my incompetent English. I am studyin' on scholarship and will return as a junior to a boardin' high school near Houston. As you can witness, I am still in the learnin' stage."

My mouth falls open. I want to hug this knotty, sincere boy who's wearing way cool John Lennon glasses. My personal translator! A Vietnamese who speaks superproper English with a Texas accent. You can't make this up.

"Hey, I'm Mia, oops, I guess I'm Mai here. Thank you, thank you, there's so much I want to say. First, please tell Út I'm so sorry."

Bless him, he doesn't ask about what but just does his job. Út answers by blowing air out her nose in a quick puff. What does that mean? She has yet to open her mouth. Bet you anything she hates her braces. Wearing them is a two-year torment, but I'm not about to walk around for the rest of my life with the top row parasailing over the bottom one. Might as well wear my braces loud and proud.

"Xin lỗi," I add for extra sorriness. Út nose-puffs again. I'm going to take that as forgiveness. Onward.

"Could you ask Út if that's a frog or a toad?"

He asks. Then the longest answer in Vietnamese: *"Only a know-nothing can't tell a frog from a toad! As misdirected as not knowing a horse from a mule. Tell her frogs belong to the family Ra-ni-dae and live in water; they lay eggs there in clusters, the tadpoles hatch, then turn into frogs with webbed feet. Toads belong to the family Bu-fo-ni-dae and live on land. They're bumpy, cracked, scary. I found mine when he was just an egg that somehow broke from a cluster in Cô Hạnh's pond. I've raised him myself."*

Translation: "Út thanks you for your inquiry and would like to inform you that she has a frog."

What a pain that Út is! But I make myself smile and nod as if I didn't understand every word the little snot said. We're even in my eyes. I'm done being sorry. For now, I'll keep my listening skills to myself.

I walk toward them and, with the biggest smile, accept the baskets of food.

I have to say Anh before Minh to show respect that he's older. The Vietnamese are all about respect. Anh Minh, it turns out, matches Mom as a superplanner. Is this also a Vietnamese thing? All I did was show him the dead phone and he whipped into must-do mode. He says we can't charge it at a more modern house because it's rude to visit relatives during nap time. His group had meant to leave the baskets on the porch, but I was awake so they stayed. We can't charge at his or the girls' homes because if they go there, they might have to nap. Not to worry, he has other plans for my cell.

"Why aren't you napping?" I ask.

"Between the ages of fifteen and fifty, some of us are too

burdened with studyin' or workin' to be nappin'."

I love that Texas accent rolling off his tongue. Come to think of it, all those between fifteen and fifty at mine and Bà's welcoming party were girls and women. Anh Minh is the first boy I've seen.

"Where are all the boys and men?" I ask.

"At our shrimp camp."

I'm imagining a summer sleepaway, where boys become men while hatching shrimps and learning the ecosystem of ocean life and mastering the fine points of canoeing and swimming and bonding.

"Whatever you are thinkin', miss, I am afraid you are mistaken. Walk and I shall explain."

I make my face blank, pretending I've been imagining an empty gray box.

Anh Minh leads, gallantly leaning his umbrella over my head and forsaking shade for himself. I tell him I'm protected by spf on steroids, but he won't listen. Hatless Út follows, with no one offering to shade her maxed-out bronze complexion. She doesn't seem to care. The two older girls go last, giggling and whispering under their umbrellas.

"Our village has joined together to buy a shrimp hatchin' facility by the sea," Anh Minh says. "The men who do not want or cannot get jobs in the city or in the government live and work there, and boys who do not pass the rigorous test into a city high school train there. That way no male finds idle time."

"What if someone doesn't like shrimp work?"

Anh Minh looks at me like I've asked the most illogical question ever. I could defend myself, but why annoy the one person who can make village life easier? I lean into his umbrella and look up and smile at his serious, sincere face.

We're walking in this maze where one-story rectangular houses are built close together, separated by waist-high cement walls. Once in a while, a many-story rectangular house pops up, separated by head-high walls. People really like cement here, pouring it in front and back to create yards. It does make sense to not coax grass out of the ground, then mow and fertilize and obsess about it. Mom's big thing is no lawns. Each house we have bought has a smaller patch of grass, the current one the size of a crib. An automatic sprinkler is forever drowning the yellowing patch. Maybe soon all of us in desert-dry Southern Cal will be graduating to all-cement yards too.

Finally, we're out on a dusty path where swampy rice paddies line each side. I'm so close I could reach down and pluck a rice stalk. But what if I fall in and go nostril to nostril with a water buffalo? I still love them, but from afar.

The red dust kicks up and sticks between my toes in my sandals. Everyone else is wearing flip-flops, which somehow let the dust fly about and rest back on the path. I'm beginning to think Mom has no clue how to dress here.

At an intersection, Anh Minh points to a gigantic tree where roots hang from thick, muscular branches. The tree obviously has roots underground, but other roots droop down and grow into the soil. The spaces in between the hanging roots create natural hiding spots, where I bet kids spend all their time when not napping.

"This tree has outlived every other livin' thing in the village. We guess it could be three hundred years old." Anh Minh glows while saying that, then he actually puts his palms together and bows at the tree. I might as well do it too. Is bowing to trees a Vietnamese thing?

Village life is centered around the tree. In one corner stands a faded, mossy pagoda, its door wide open in the heat. Inside, on tile, dozens of dogs with lolling tongues lie half asleep. Among the dogs and their spilled water bowls, a duck is waddling, sipping here and there. Somehow, perfectly natural.

We head to the opposite corner of the pagoda and into an open market, closed for nap time. Merchants have put newspapers over their goods and handkerchiefs over their faces and are sleeping and snoring on cots spread out next to their stalls. It's like walking through a Vietnamese-village version of Sleeping Beauty frozen under the witch's spell.

I like the quiet.

We walk deeper into the market and stop in front of what looks like a cement hut with a door and no window. I'm wondering what goods are stored in there when Anh Minh makes that open-palm swing to mean "go in." Seeing my alarmed face, he explains, "It is an internet café."

Okay, let's not say "café." You would imagine coffee and muffins and soft lighting and sleepy music and you would be wrong. Imagine instead a hot shack with a tin roof that makes it even hotter and two old computers on DIAL-UP, that's right, DIAL-UP, but I can charge the cell. Thank you, universe. We have time, so I pay the equivalent of ten cents for the slowest internet connection ever.

I log on. After an eternity, I get twenty-nine messages. Some from Mom. Each with an inspirational message about hanging in there and a new SAT word for the day. DELETE, DELETE, DELETE. Being across the world rocks! Most from Montana. A crisis about tan lines, a crisis about too-glossy lip glosses, a crisis about choosing a French, lobster-tail, or waterfall braid. DELETE, DELETE, DELETE. There's an FB notification from Montana. I log on and wait. Mia Le. Weird to see that name. I haven't been her in a while.

OMG, on my wall is a tagged pic of her and HIM at Anita, a beach where almost-teens go to get away from moms and little kids. I click over to her wall. Wait. And wait. Finally, I'm in. More photos, all bikini shots. Did she Photoshop to make her boobs look extra big? How big do they need to be? I don't want her boobs, but I have to confess I do want the attention they get her. Does that make me pathetic and sophomoric?

There HE is, just as I suspected, standing right behind her butt bow. She's smiling over her shoulder. I know that smirk. HE's not smiling back though, kinda looking up, way up. I scroll down and it says HE and she friended the day I left. That means she asked HIM. Still, HE shouldn't have accepted.

What's wrong with me? HE can do whatever. Beads of sweat, mixed with sunblock, slide into my eyes, letting me cry a little.

But I can't indulge and throw myself down. Anh Minh and the girls are standing behind me, not sweaty, but definitely misty, eyes on the screen, looking at the beach photographs. I would give anything to have an hour alone.

Anh Minh, seeing me see him, pretends like he hasn't been staring at the screen and flips his concentration to the tin roof, like it reveals some unsolved theorem. He's already told me he's going to be a mathematician/professor/poet. Please, universe, never let my mother meet him. I can just hear her comparisons and sighs.

Út is twisting her mouth and gearing up for questions about Montana, no doubt. I kick my expression into neutral, but my heart is pumping blood to my face. Stop it, feelings, do not show that I'm flustered having seen evidence of Montana and HIM together. I have no idea if my feelings are listening.

The two older girls keep whispering to each other. I've never actually heard them speak. Anh Minh straightens himself, so grateful to have translation to do.

"Who's she with breasts so full?" So begins the froggy one.

"My friend Montana."

"Why is she older in age?"

"She's twelve, my age."

"Twelve? And a baby she has?" Út won't stop with the questions.

"What baby?"

"Her breasts swell for no reason?"

"Believe me, she has reasons."

"Are you certain she's twelve? Did she fail some grades?"

"She's twelve, I told you."

"Are breasts the size of human heads admired in America?"

How can one person be this nosy? I think, but say, "Not her fault they're that size."

"She has to stuff them into tiny triangles?"

"It's Southern California. People wear bikinis to the beach."

"Must she call attention to her buttocks also? Is she trying to mate? But the males are the ones to court the females."

"She's not a duck or a peacock. She's my best friend. She's smart in her own way. She's very happy, really."

"Best friend? She would think of your happiness before her own?"

I make myself nod slowly. I don't know why I'm defending Montana, but I feel like if I don't, my life will fall apart. Út is a pain, pain, pain. I'm in no mood to be interrogated. What does Út know? She's obsessed with a gargantuan frog.

I always talk really fast when agitated, as if words could drown out anxieties. On and on I blab about how Montana and I are borderline teenagers and that means pressure and change and freedom and bodies. I forget to pause to let Anh Minh translate. There's so much to say about becoming a teenager. The more I talk, the more I can fake calmness. HE was looking away from her butt bow, right? I would be able to tell in two seconds if I were standing right there. Dad could not have picked a worse summer for his must-please-my-momma project. My mind obsesses about HIM while my mouth spews out teen facts. Is this what they mean by "split personality"? When I do pause, Anh Minh seems stumped.

"There's no word for teenager in Vietnamese, miss. Numbers in English go from ten to eleven to twelve, then thirteen, fourteen.

So the jump from twelve to thirteen has cultural plus spellin' ramifications. But in Vietnamese, we say ten, then ten one, ten two, ten three, ten four, so there's no change. Literally, a teenager would start at ten and that has no meanin' here or over there. The closest we have here is *tuổi dậy-thì*, which is the age of puberty at fifteen, sixteen."

"Just tell them it's a big deal to go from twelve to thirteen."

"They won't believe me because there's no such change here."

What is the point of having a personal translator if he's going to argue with me about facts, actual facts. Everybody knows turning thirteen is a gigantic marker, the way old people remember where they were when Kennedy was shot or, for the Vietnamese, where they were the day Saigon fell.

What were my parents thinking, dumping me in a place where teenagers do not exist, where every single person eats some form of rice for every single meal, where napping is a public event, where perfectly well-behaved kids are banished from real conversations?

The worst part? No one here would listen to my many, many, many complaints. No one even complains.

CHAPTER 8

Anh Minh walks me back to Bà. After blabbermouth Út went off somewhere, the older girls giggled and also left. Anh Minh looked longingly after one of them. He reminds me of myself. The sassy hip-shaker is like Montana, and Chị Lan is like HIM, the one who gets to choose. Why is my most secret heartache being replicated in a love triangle in a tiny Vietnamese village?

The sun, still scorching, is sinking toward midafternoon, almost wake-up time. We pass back through the market and, like in a cartoon, handkerchiefs rise and fall over the faces of snoring merchants. At first, it's embarrassing to witness something so private, but after a while it makes perfect sense that people who spend all their waking moments together would also synchronize their naps.

I wonder if anyone ever feels lonely here. Earlier, when we

walked by a four-story house, I heard Út say if she were home alone in such a huge house she would be scared of ghosts. Strange coming from Út, who seems impervious to everything. But I guess if you're used to constant company, that much silent space would be creepy.

As we enter my courtyard, the cell rings. Anh Minh bows and leaves.

"What took so long?" is Mom's sleepy hello. My muscles instantly relax. Yes, the perfect person to complain to.

"You have no idea how crazy busy they keep me here. Every second, something is expected of me. People are everywhere. I never have a second alone. There's no outlet in the house, so I about died of a heatstroke going to charge the phone."

"Let's start over. How are you, sweetie?"

"Terrible. I couldn't be worse. It's hot and muggy and I've got enough mosquito bites to do an elaborate dot-to-dot, and my pants are all wrong and my sandals are all wrong and my clingy shirt makes me hotter and I don't know why I'm being punished."

"Mai."

There she goes again, saying my name in a way that can't help but be soothing. I don't want to be soothed.

"Mai, love. What is it?"

"Everything. I hate it here. Why did you make me come? It's not fair. I didn't do anything wrong. I can't help that Bà's husband got taken away in THE WAR. Why is it on me to make it right? I'm just a kid. I want to go home."

"Mai, deep breath in, now out. I'm sorry, I should have packed long, loose pants and lots of anti-itch ointment. But I know a trick for mosquito bites. Rub your own saliva on the bump to counteract the anticoagulant that the mosquito released when it bit you. But it must be your own to stop the itch, not someone else's."

"Mother! I would never slobber my spit over myself! Why would you even suspect I might use someone else's?"

"My, you're in a mood. Is this about him? Is he with Montana?"

My insides turn to liquid, surging a gigantic tidal wave of nausea into my throat. I literally drop the phone. The ground spins. I plop down on the dirt and squeeze my head between my knees. Why does my life have to suck this much? How did Mom guess that I liked someone? Have I been visibly pining? I'm afraid to ask. I breathe in and out, in and out. The phone is getting dusty. I pick it up and polish it; after all, it's my one link to real life. I stand up. Mom is still yakking on and on.

"At times, being away is the best test. If he's truly worthwhile, sweetie, he'll be here when you get back. It's a test for you and Montana too. What do you want in a friend? Besides, you have a lifetime for boys, why not enjoy your summer with Bà and see what will surprise you?"

The only thing worse than Mom guessing my most private, private thought is her using every cliché to advise me about it. Did I talk in my sleep? How does she guess exactly what I've been thinking, even when I didn't want to think it? What do I want in a friend? If that question doesn't breed a panic attack, I don't know what will. First, bossy Út asked if Montana would put my happiness before hers, now this pep talk from Mom. I wish people would stop stomping around in my head.

"Mai? Say something, help me stay awake. It's about midnight here. I've had you on automatic dial every hour since we last talked. Are you all right? Say something."

"Something."

"Now, now. When you're ready to talk, I'm here. I'm always here even if I'm not right next to you. I got international calling plans so we can talk anytime."

"I hear Bà," I lie, but it's about the time when Bà would wake and want her tea.

"What if we talk again when I'm up? That's our only real chance because tomorrow will be a trying day in court. That should be around ten at night for you. Can you stay up?"

"Maybe."

"Before I forget, SAT word for today, conundrum, c-o-n-u—"

My finger somehow holds down OFF. Oops.

That's it. I'm on an SAT revolt, erasing all five-dollar words from my cobwebby mind. Expunged, good-bye. Wait, is *expunge* an SAT word? Probably. Rewind. How about *zapped*? Zapped, good-bye. It'll kill Mom when I come back espousing the vocabulary of a middle schooler, which I am. Wait, is *espouse* SAT? I'm going to have to be vigilant. *Vigilant?* OMG, Mom has completely warped me.

I keep the phone off, ostensibly to save the battery. But I can't handle Mom just yet. She will try too hard to help and will drive me batty. No one, not even Mom, can fix my gargantuan problems. Other than flying home right now and rolling Montana in a rug and stashing the rug in a garage, I don't know what anyone can do. I don't even know if HE likes her, or me, or someone else, or anyone at all. It doesn't help that I'm stuck in a mosquitoey swamp on the other side of the world. Where is that quack detective?

Of course it's pouring. We would have to visit during the rainy season, when, in addition to being hot and muggy, which mosquitoes love, there are also downpours to provide puddle nurseries. Every time one mosquito sucks a hint of my blood, she has the nutrients to have zillions of babies. So glad I could help.

Bà and I and Ông's Brother are in the front room, drinking tea by the window, watching arrow-like raindrops puncture the cement courtyard. There's no talking. We sip and stare, sip and stare.

I'm supposed to call him Ông Thuận. Bà wrote down the name and pronounced it over and over. But I can't simultaneously pucker my lips, twist my tongue, push the vowels front to back really fast, flip my intestines, and close my throat. So I keep calling him "Ông's Brother." Predictable, but how inventive can I be when I'm this distraught? When all I can think about is how often has Montana's butt bow been menacing HIM? And how long has Mom known about HIM?

We've had three refills when Ông's Brother starts talking. Startled, I nearly spill scorching tea on my lap. That's all I need to make this day perfect, a third-degree burn.

Ông's Brother points to a huge wooden block mounted on a thick tree stump. He tells us that long ago Ông built this square birdhouse, each side carved with four perfect circular nests, which have never been empty of doves.

"Years ago, I took a pair of doves to the mountain on my yearly search for ginseng," Ông's Brother says. *"I released them, thinking they would crave the wild, but they returned before I did."*

"It's impossible to forget the core of one's being."

"Even if lost, I sensed they never would have relinquished finding a way home."

"Unless something intruded."

"He would have returned if he could."

"What might have prevented him?"

"Even without knowing, we can provide him with a proper place to rest."

"Rest?"

"His spot in the family plot still awaits, as yours. I myself have rested a son there. His body was lost in the war, but his spirit I buried at home."

"How did you know the moment to release waiting?"

"After the war ended, I hoped. Every day I looked into the horizon for his frame. Soldier after soldier returned, on feet shredded like cloth, on bicycles of dented wheels and without tires, they returned from the lowest tip of the South. Each year fewer came home. By the third year, I saw nothing but dust in the horizon. Day after day. Then his mother stepped into the next life and took him with her, side by side."

Bà nods. Ông's Brother looks deeper into the horizon. They return to silence. I understood every word, but somehow the meaning is as impossible to hold as each drop of rain.

As quickly as the rain slammed down, it suddenly thins to brushstrokes. Bà stands up and walks toward the birdhouse, her head uncovered, striding with purpose. She will get damp, enough to chill her. I scramble after her. Right then, the doves fly out of the birdhouse, and by some invisible cue, they hover above us with white wings wide, creating a feathery, rhythmic umbrella.

Bà traces each circle on the birdhouse, sixteen in all. I know she's thinking Ông's own hands had carved these circles. Somehow, that makes him more real to me. Ông walked this village; he slept in the blue goddess room; he ate grapefruit from the garden tree. I trace each circle too.

Bà starts a long, murmuring chant. I listen, not to actual words but to their undeniable weight.

I'm all set to hate it here, then something magical has to happen.

CHAPTER 9

I'm pinching myself to stay awake. Twenty-three more minutes until midnight, which will be 10:00 a.m. the day before in Laguna, the time Montana should be up but not yet at the beach.

All night I've planned as much as possible, channeling efficient Mom. I borrowed a pair of Bà's pajamas, saying I want to be comfortable, and they are supercomfortable, but really I need to cover as much skin as possible so I can talk outside without bloodsuckers devouring me. I practice sounding light and fun, like I'm calling to check in. I have to make sure I do not slip and mention HIM, even though I hope Montana will refer to HIM in an offhanded, flighty way. Montana doesn't have Mom's power to X-ray thoughts, so my secret is safe.

I do feel guilty having missed Mom's call at 10:00 p.m., the phone vibrating like a silent scream. Mom texted and texted, but it was a perfectly believable time to be asleep. Bà was. Mom must be worried, her mind automatically imagines the worst. I don't know how long I can avoid her. But she would have interrogated me, plucking out each little bit about HIM. The sad truth is we barely have bits. We know who each other is and have said hi, that's about it. HE's always been around, but I didn't notice HIM at school until a few months ago when HE talked about a love poem in class. HIS face softened to reveal a look of longing I grew up seeing in Bà.

It's time. I crawl out with Bà's socks on. That leaves just my hands and face exposed. Surely, I can jiggle to protect three little areas. I rush past the birdhouse, all the way to the grapefruit tree at the farthest edge of the garden.

I punch 001 before Montana's number, harder to do than you'd think while jiggling. She's supposed to have memorized my number too, in case an earthquake happens and we have to call from someone's phone. But I have a feeling she memorized as far as the area code.

"Mont, it's me."

"Is it really you? I can just die. It's been so weird without you. I can't believe it's really you. You have no idea how wrong my life is right now. Like yesterday, Hadley was over, and I could not for the life of me teach her the lobster tail. Then she just put on my favorite lip gloss, without even asking, then she was all 'I don't like the smell.' Can you believe that? She's shuttling in any minute and I swear I'm done, like done done. I think she likes that boy in English class, you know, the one who talked about that poem . . ."

I know exactly which boy, my boy. The familiar tidal wave of nausea. I fight it by pacing. Forget standing still and jiggling, I've got to pace to buffer against mosquitoes and dread. "You can't be at the beach already, with Hadley?"

"Yeah, I said I didn't like her but you always have, so I'm, like, fine."

"You know I'm calling from across the world. You know I didn't call to talk about Hadley."

"Guess who's here?"

"Why are you at the beach at ten in the morning?"

"It was supposed to be so awesome, a huge pod of dolphins was spotted really early, but by the time we got here . . . Hey, you can't be leaving?"

"Me? No."

"Not you. I'm talking to Poet Dude. Hadley is all wrong for him, don't you think? Hey, come here, stop walking away, talk to Mia, she's calling all the way from Vietnam, that's where she's from. . . ."

I didn't think it was possible, but I feel sicker than I did just a minute ago. I'm clutching the phone so hard the veins on my hand pop. I pace, fast. Montana is telling HIM what a great idea my trip is, as if she could last a day here. She's babbling, meaning she's nervous. We have that sad trait in common.

"Talk to her, talk to Mia," she keeps saying, like she's in sales.

Her breathing gets louder. She must be running after HIM.

"Hey."

I stop pacing, knowing that "hey" well. There's no mistaking the speaker.

"Hey," I manage. That came out dry and pained, as if an army of ants were crawling down my throat.

"What's it like there?" HIS first sentence directed at me, ever. What a beautiful sentence.

"Hot." Have the ants eaten all my words? The mosquitoes sure are. Jiggle, jiggle.

"Here too. We're in the middle . . ."

I hear scratchy noises, then we're cut off. Why, why, why? HE was talking to me. And I was getting ready to talk back. I redial and get voice mail. I call again. Voice mail. I text. Wait. No response. Being across the world sucks.

How can a conversation lasting 2 minutes, 12.8 seconds leave me this jittery? What just happened?

HE and I exchanged words. Excellent.

HE was trying to walk away from Montana. Good.

Montana was nervous, that means she's plotting for HIS attention. Dangerous.

Hadley likes HIM, that means Montana will try even harder. Dire.

Montana didn't ask one question about my trip or say that she misses me. Rude.

If only I could confide in Montana and get her to fish around for

HIS feelings for me, but that's never going to happen. Depressing.

So many emotions are crashing into one another that my whole body hurts. I run into the house. Things will clear up when I'm rested and energized. They have to, right?

CHAPTER 10

Tense voices wake me up. Bà's and a man's. Not Ông's Brother. Definitely not Anh Minh. Not Dad's. I wish. OMG, it's our detective.

I scramble out of the net, which is harder to do than you'd think, and run into the front room. He's here, as leathery and wordy as ever. I've only marked four days off my Trip of Torment calendar. This man is a genius. I will be at the beach blocking HIM from Montana's butt bow very soon, la la la. Then I look around. Wait, where's the guard?

I look at Bà with a desperate expression that surely conveys, "Where's the guard?" but Bà just frowns.

"Please forgive my granddaughter, she has not awakened enough to employ her manners," Bà says to him. To me, *"Your clothes?"*

As if her pajama-ish matching silk set looks that different from my real pajamas matching silk set. But I obviously do not possess the magical powers to tell loose day wear from loose night wear. I go change, returning in proper mosquito-bait capris. Bà shakes her head just the slightest bit. I get it. Go outside, away from adult conversation.

Not to worry, I have major spying skills. They're talking in the front room, so by squatting outside under the open window I can hear everything. I used chopsticks to place a rotting banana under the window. In position, plastic bag in hand, I can always say I'm catching fruit flies for you-know-who.

I only understand Bà's part of the conversation. When the detective talks, his words float away then pop like bubbles. He, unfortunately, does most of the talking. I have to bounce while squatting to keep my legs from going to sleep. I do realize how weird I look.

"You have located the guard in Hà Nội? Why isn't he here?"

Pop, pop, pop.

"I will not go to him. I need rest. He held my husband captive; he must come to me to release his past."

Pop, pop, pop.

"This man is pointing at the sun when the answer resides at his feet. No one will think he is profiting from the war. Every detail, every drop, means . . ."

More pops. Ugh!

"Tell him I've waited through the war, through the maturity of seven children, through a foreign world, waited for the day when

someone can reveal how my husband absorbed the air without his family beside him. Tell him we will not talk of war. It simply was. Better yet, tell him I want to listen, no more."

The detective takes a long breath, as if to slow down his whole being. *"I will explain your story again."*

Wow, I understand him! He is capable of normal talk. Maybe Bà should numb him more often with the facts of her life. But where's the guard? That's the question I want the answer to.

"Miss, what are you doin'?"

I jump and wham my head under the half-open shutter. Double OOOWWWW! My translator is the coolest ever, but I could use some alone time, thank you. He's going to ask why don't I use the bathroom instead of squatting and bouncing. If I ran into me right now, I would ask exactly that. Quickly, I hold up my pathetic bag imprisoning three fruit flies. Those tiny things rarely need to land.

"Surely, you are not goin' to all this trouble for Frog? He is so enormous we are all fearful he will have a heart attack. Can you imagine the catastrophic response from Miss Út?"

I make a big show of standing up and releasing the captured three, for the sake of obese pets everywhere.

Now Bà and the detective are in front of the house. I oh-so-casually ease my way over there. Sly, that's me.

Bà nods and heads inside. I smile really big at the detective, pretending mega interest so I can find out the deal with the guard.

"Chào Anh," I say, and bow toward the detective, so proud I can greet him all by myself.

Anh Minh laughs. “Miss, he is your grandfather’s age so you must address him as Ông.”

“I thought my Ông is called Ông.”

“When you say ‘Ông’ alone everyone knows you mean your grandfather. But when you address someone of the same generation you must say Ông plus the man’s first name.”

The detective clutches my hand and says, *“Ông Ba nắm chặt tay con, dù cho chiến-tranh đã chia rẽ nhiều người, dù rằng nhiều tim đã thành miếng đá, Ông Ba từ lâu đã quyết-định rằng. . . .”*

What is he saying about my grandparents?

My translator steps in. “His name is Ông Ba. Ba means three, thus he ranks as the third son in his family. Different from Ông Bà where your tone goes downward for Bà.”

I must look confused because Anh Minh repeats, *“Ông Ba,”* pointing at the detective and *“Ông Bà,”* pointing at Bà inside the house. I DO NOT HEAR ANY DIFFERENCE!

Anh Minh just won’t stop. “Ba, Bà, as distinctive as saying choose chose.”

Show-off! I shoot him my famous laser-death stare.

“If you allow me, miss, I would like to teach you the diacritical marks. Once you know how to pronounce them, and there are only nine for the twelve main vowels and the various ways to combine them, you will know how to say every word perfectly because the beauty of Vietnamese stems from every word bein’ spelled exactly the way it sounds. You will never mispronounce like a foreigner again.”

"I sound like a foreigner?"

"Uh, not . . . hum, barely . . ."

Just then Ông Bà, I mean Ông Ba, oh forget it, I'll just go right back to calling him "the detective," opens his mouth and releases ribbons of bubbles.

Anh Minh listens so intently veins start pulsating at his temples. "Miss, I apologize but I cannot fully translate his true words. They are beyond my humble English. Not to worry, I will persevere."

That said, Anh Minh whips out a notebook and pen from his back pocket and takes notes. Of course the international scholar would have a notebook and pen ready. I bet he has a calculator on him too. On second thought, he probably calculates everything in his head. Seeing the notebook, the wordy, leathery one lets it all pop. Anh Minh looks like he's listening to a love song, scribbling, scribbling. They deserve each other.

I might as well go inside.

Bà is sitting by the window, eating *cháo*, a hot rice porridge, this one cooked with catfish and dill, Bà's favorite breakfast. A covered bowl waits for me. *Cháo*, not to be confused with *chào*, meaning hello, is starting to be my favorite too, light and savory. I'm jiggling my legs to keep away you-know-what. Bà wants to laugh but she's always too polite.

Of course Bà would never worry about the buzzers craving

her blood, pure and bland from decades of greens and grains. Anh Minh told me mosquitoes here love overseas visitors, whose blood is loaded with sugar. He said it like that's a universal fact. True, mine has been doused with Hawaiian bread and cereal and corn chips and just plain corn, all of which you wouldn't think have tons of sugar, but according to Mom, eating them is like spooning white sugar straight into your mouth. Well, I haven't been eating any invisible sugars here (I don't think), but the mosquitoes still adore me. How long before my blood turns salty?

I'm fitting Vietnamese words together to ask about the guard, but it's taking forever because I can only speak like thirty words. My listening brain and my speaking brain do not like to share.

Bà notices, of course. She pats my hand and gives me that smile, the one that says she would give me the world if she could.

"Con khổ." I'm suffering, I tell her. *"Không chịu được,"* can't bear it.

Bà takes my hand. *"Shsss, không sao,"* not to worry. She's said it a million times, and each time I do feel better. *"When you can complain out loud, I know you're still strong. When your pain has advanced beyond lament, when it's unbearable to hear your own story, that's when I know to truly worry. Though hidden in silence, your pain would still surface on your breaths, your eyes, your pores. I will know. Take long inhales, my child, you are more bendable than you realize."*

I have no idea if I'm bendable or not, I just want to go home.

"Muốn về," want home, I finally say it out loud. She nods the saddest nod.

"I know friends build your world at this age, you must miss them so. My child, lend me a bit more of your time. I am overjoyed you are by my side. Yet if my asking equals suffering, we have the option of contacting your father to begin arrangements to release you of your obligation."

I shrivel to a speck of dust. What kind of a granddaughter would I be if I zip home when this is the only task Bà has ever asked of me? To load on the guilt, she looks anguished, truly anguished, for my pain.

"Không sao," no worries, I hear myself say. I don't quite believe it, but Bà has always been able to soothe me with these two words. *"Không sao,"* I say again, more for her than for me. The words work their magic because her cheekbones pump up into the bottom of her eyes.

"Chờ được không?" Can you wait? she asks.

I make myself nod yes, before honesty takes over.

We eat in silence. I chant *"không sao"* to myself over and over. Perhaps after a while, I will wholeheartedly believe it'll be all right to wait. What can I do but wait? Things will happen in Laguna whether I stress or not. I wish I could force myself to stop thinking about HIM or Montana or the beach until I'm actually home. I hate waiting. Who wouldn't? Especially when I have no idea how long the wait is. Is it still around two weeks? The detective coming here, twisty-browed and whispery, cannot be a good sign. That's the worst part, not knowing. I don't even know how to find out because I bet nobody knows. The only person who can wait for decades in absolute stillness is Bà.

She pushes her bowl away and asks if I'd like a story. When I was little, she'd tell me a story when I was sad. I've always loved her stories, even if they're sadder than anything I could be feeling. I love the way she pulls words into a tight embrace.

"They came in white uniforms, the same crisp pants and hard-brimmed hat that Ông had always worn. The men came and stood hats in hands, eyes in the distance. They had to wrestle words from clogged throats. I heard clearly: 'is now recorded as missing in action.'

"That day was the tenth in April, year of the horse 1966.

"Later, when we fled war and country, I needed a birth day and month to request refuge. Your father and aunts and uncles knew their dates of birth, having grown up when the world tilted toward the West. I had remained planted in the East where the lunar year and the exact hour of entrance into this world marked a person's fate.

"No one could enter the United States without a date of birth, a space for that was reserved on every single form. There were endless forms. I was not the only one to stare at the blank spaces. Someone advised us to choose a date readily remembered.

"The tenth day in each April.

"The date stabbed me every time I was required to record it. This guaranteed continued remembrance. I didn't choose the last day I saw him. That day remains solely mine.

"I had reached out, just as Ông was leaving, to align the rim of his straw hat. He was not in uniform that day but dressed as a casual traveler. As if a change of clothes could camouflage fate. That day he went on a mission on Route 1, straight toward the claws of the Communists.

"When I reached out I might have grazed my palm against his cheek. Our last touch. I'm no longer certain if we indeed met skin to skin those many years ago, and despite the years I have not been able to release the possibility.

"I did not borrow a date of birth from your father or his siblings. Seven of them. Whose date would be best? To confess, the exact birth day and month of each child have never attached to my memories, though the year and hour of each have long become a part of my breaths.

"Ông named each child after the closing line he wrote in every letter home. Written in the years when he was in a French school while I was being tutored at home. In the years before the Việt Minh turned its head and revealed the tail of the Việt Cộng while I was a youthful mother. In the year when the navy trained him in San Di-e-go while I managed our house and brood.

"Always his letters closed with Mong Nhớ Em Đếm Từng Hạt Mưa. *This line was written in his very first letter home in the voice of a lonely boy sent to the city, a boy who stared at the spring rain as he longed for his bride-in-waiting.*

"The names embarrassed our children, your father especially. How could we have named a boy after drops the shape of tears, he argued? I had offered alternatives after each birth, but Ông clung to

these names like roots to the earth. He wanted to look at his children and be struck by the core of his feelings in our times apart."

I've always laughed at the names of Ông Bà's children. *Mong Nhớ Em Đếm Từng Hạt Mưa* means Longing Missing You Counting Each Drop of Rain. C'mon, who names their children after a sappy line in a letter? It's romantic and all, but death on playgrounds. It's even worse when attached to a title. Uncle Longing. Uncle Missing. Aunt You. Aunt Counting. Aunt Each. Uncle Drop. Daddy Rain.

Not that Montana's parents did much better. Montana has an older sister named Wyoming. That was when their dad was into the wild, wild West and bought a horse ranch. A movie producer, he then figured out he didn't know anything about and didn't care for horses. Montana said he switched interest to his assistant, and they had a baby boy named People. For real, People. So Montana's mom moved to Laguna and bought the grandest house she could find.

When I'm furious with Daddy Rain, I call him Thunder, Cloud, Typhoon, Monsoon. But just in my head. Dad has no sense of humor about this. When he got to the United States, Dad tried going by Rain, but that led to many problems among middle schoolers. So he came up with Ray, which has no connection to his given name but gave him some peace. At home, though, he has always been Mưa.

CHAPTER 11

Everything is still in shadows, and the really loud rooster next door hasn't even started crowing yet, but I might as well get up. It doesn't help that a constant seesawing snore blasts from the back room. The detective is staying over because he and Bà talked late into the night. All that talking and I know nothing more. If it had been my choice, I would have shooed him out the door to go do his job. But I have very little say in life right now.

All yesterday the detective ignored me and catered to Bà, who asked me to wait. I've been waiting! Dad sent word through Mom that a patient has had extreme complications and he can't return to sort out the problem with the guard for a while. How long is "for a while"? Mom texted this news because she was in court and couldn't talk. I dutifully texted her back saying the phone part isn't working, but texting is fine. By texting, I can ignore her questions about a "friend." Just imagining talking to Mom about HIM turns my stomach into a wave pool. In return, Mom ignored how I ended each text with "I wnt 2 go hme." Texting, though, didn't prevent her from leaving exasperated voice messages. I get that she's worried, but I can't talk to her. Not yet.

I'm forever creating possibilities in my crazed mind. One, Montana and HE somehow are together, and that will end my obsession. I'm not going to keep liking someone who goes for Montana. Two, they are not together, so I maneuver a way to find out how HE feels about me, but this will encourage Montana if she knows I like HIM. OMG, this one topic has ballooned in my mind for months and I'm right back to square one? I'm starting to bore myself, although I'm still really interested.

I force myself to get up.

I step onto the porch in Bà's pajamas and socks. Whoa, it's actually cool out. Not beach breezes but for once the air is not nibbling at my skin like thousands of miniature insects. Shadows are moving about. A hint of morning comes from the east, from California.

I love Laguna in June. That's when we get this marine layer that covers the air in a gray, cool fog all morning. Montana hates it, saying all that grayness is depressing. Oh, but the air is so cool it's like standing in water while keeping dry. I made a habit of getting up really early and sitting on the back porch, soaking up the fog until it burned off. If I was lucky, the fog wouldn't lift at all and I would float among gray clouds all day.

My favorites are the days when you can literally watch the fog crawl in from the ocean. We're up the hill, so I get to see thick puffs of white smoke expand into a blanket, hovering above downtown. It looks solid enough to walk on.

HE's there, probably downhill skating too fast, curls whipping onto HIS helmet, eyes screaming behind sunglasses even on a cloudy day.

"Good mornin', miss."

I jump, squealing a little. My translator has got to stop sneaking up on me.

"Why are you up?"

"I never slept. I have the grandest surprise for you."

"Let me guess. . . . Út wants to be my best friend and give me her obese pet?"

Anh Minh laughs. Even without sleep he's upstanding, a shadow of shiny teeth and bright eyes, behind glasses no less. Is that much good mood good for you?

"What you are suggestin' is, how do you say it, a tall inquisition? I have been up all night doin' a much more humble task."

He means a tall order, but I can't correct him. He's beyond corrections.

He unfolds pieces of paper, dark with tiny writing. I swear he gets his spine to straighten up even higher. Bet he rocks at every single class presentation. Of course he has a flashlight, making him the most prepared high schooler on earth.

"You look more Vietnamese in a matching outfit."

"Really?"

"I would never lie, miss."

He's so earnest, all I can say is "I know." I'm going to try my best to be good-natured like him.

"Now listen, this is what Ông Ba told me: 'Ordinarily, the sorrow of her grandmother's magnitude, rankin' deeper than most familial displacement that war induces, touchin' upon the tenderness of unrequited longin', would, and should, sprout utmost empathy from even those whose hearts have deadened. And yet, I am deeply ashamed and shocked to report, the man with knowledge of her grandfather's lonely days has refused all proper invitations to appear before the one who awaits his words most.'"

"The detective is even wordier in translation. How is that possible?" I ask.

"Miss, allow me to continue, it gets really good. 'Let it be known that it was I who first found him, after searchin' every alley and crevice of our beloved country durin' its shattered remains after war and for years while the land and its people recovered. Indeed, it was I who rolled in every dusty corner, tracked down every friend, neighbor, office worker who knew her grandfather. He was an effusive man, capable of much laughter and friends. I needed years to complete the task.'"

"When exactly does it get good?"

"This is pertinent information about your grandmother. Listen. 'In an extension of what her grandmother already knew, I found three men who also shared that unfortunate day with your grandfather but were later released. All were kept in Củ Chị, a district infamous for enemy infiltration underneath the earth, as this was where the Communists dug tunnels and fought like moles during the war. I came to know the district as well as the lines on the palms of my hands. One day, while stoppin' for a sugarcane beverage to offset the notorious heat and dust of the area, as few vegetation had regrown after the brutal wartime strategy of droppin' chemicals that killed anythin' green and growin', I chanced upon the proprietor, the very man who had held her grandfather as a prisoner.'"

"STOOOOPPPPP! I have no idea what you're saying. My head hurts!!!!"

"Miss, I have pages of more translation."

"My brain will explode. Do you want that?"

Anh Minh deflates. He did stay up all night. Fine, I'll play nice, having just vowed to be more agreeable. "How about you answer questions? Don't read, just answer, okay?"

So polite, Anh Minh makes himself nod. He's still disappointed, but I need my head, attached.

"Where is the guard?"

"In Hà Nội."

"He's a van ride away?" I almost shout. "Doesn't he get that Bà is here just to see him?"

"It is a matter of personal integrity. He is adamant that your Bà comes to him, that no one misconstrues his goodwill for greed."

"Greed how?"

"He does not want anyone to think he is hopin' for a monetary exchange."

"Why are we putting up with him? Does he actually know anything?" Now I do shout.

"This man guarded your Ông while he was in captivity. That is more than the detective has ever tracked down," Anh Minh explains. He is patient.

"So everyone agrees that Ông is not alive, for sure?"

"I must not speak for your Bà, but it is most unlikely."

"If there's no Ông, why aren't we going home?"

"Your Bà is achin' for finality, I believe." Anh Minh sounds sad.

"Isn't Ông being truly gone final enough?"

"It is not my place to say but there is death and there is acceptance." His voice sounds even sadder. "Those two do not always conjoin in time and thought."

I think Dad said something like that, and Bà herself told me as much. I might have been so intent on going home that I missed listening.

"Exactly how long does it take to accept something?"

"That is the billion-dollar question."

I hate it when I ask a perfectly clear question and get a point to ponder in reply. Cut it out, I need an answer. Obviously, it won't come from Anh Minh. So I try an easier question. "Why can't Bà and I go to him?"

"Your dad wants him to come here so your Bà can rest. Besides, she herself says it is a matter of respect."

A sinking, sick feeling is spreading in my gut. I'm going to be stuck here forever. It won't matter if HE actually might like me because I'll be Bà's age when I finally get to go home. Neither side is going to appease the other because of something only they understand. The sickness must have spread to my face because Anh Minh panics.

"Do not worry. If anyone can find the guard and bring him here, it is your detective, miss."

"Really?"

"He is movin' the sky to do so."

I frown. That's a bit of the detective talking. "Last question: why does he stack twenty words on top of each other when one would do?"

"He has always wanted to be a poet."

The world is suddenly so tiring. I must go back to sleep, even if the loudest rooster on earth is just waking up.

CHAPTER 12

Two days later, the detective is still here, still whispering with Bà. What could he possibly be saying? Go do your job, I want to shout but can't. My curse: rebellious in my head but oh-so lovely in real life. I should call Mom and complain until my spit dries up, but talking to her means ripping out my guts about HIM. So I'm back to suffering silently and alone.

I hope the detective at least is telling Bà it might be time to accept that nothing more can be known, that just because the guard ran into Ông a long, long time ago doesn't mean he actually remembers anything important. I don't dare ask Anh Minh to translate all that because when I texted those thoughts to Mom, she about had a meltdown.

"Let Bà find acceptance her way. Do not interfere. Be thoughtful."

I wanted to reply, "I m here. U r not. Who mre thghtful?" But I held back because Mom is so cranky these days, probably not sleeping much. Yesterday, when I texted my standard "I wnt 2 go hme," she shot back, "This trip is not about you." She hasn't asked to talk for real lately, and seems actually okay just texting me. I thought I was the center of her world? And she no longer drops hints about HIM. That's Mom for you, hot and cold, hot and cold. Her trial must be sucking up her every brain cell.

Meanwhile, I've been doing nothing but eating and sleeping, which sounds amazing until that's all you get to do. I'm now an expert insect watcher, sorting flying buzzers from crawlers from danglers, then categorizing each group by shape, size, and color. So so fascinating. For more subtropical fun, I also have intimate knowledge of the sticky heat and constant noises.

You'd think a little village in North Vietnam couldn't help but be tranquil and quiet, full of banana groves and bamboo forests, but everything here has a big mouth. Dogs fighting, crickets blasting, frogs screaming, chickens clucking, birds screeching, mice scurrying . . . all this before the humans, the many many humans, add to the cacophony. I know, SAT alert. It's work getting rid of these words, work.

I'm so well fed, I can literally feel my brain cells getting plump and lazy. I'm actually not plotting anything while having breakfast on the porch with Bà and the detective. Bà keeps saying the same things and the detective keeps answering in bubble sentences. Aren't they bored? I am.

We're eating *cháo* again. It was left on the porch, and the *cháo* stayed hot in a pot encased inside a shape-fitting sweater cocooned inside the basket. Someone went through a lot of trouble for us. The detective adds so many chopped scallions to his bowl my eyes water, then he SLURPS SLURPS SLURPS through puckered lips. Next, he CHOMPS CHOMPS CHOMPS. All the while writing super-slowly in that decrepit notebook. All his private habits would be unknown to me if he were out in the world doing his job.

"Tell him in the spirit of balance he should come to me."

"If only . . ."

Please, universe, make these conversations stop.

Then Anh Minh and Út's mom, whom I call Cô Tâm to mean Aunt Tâm but I don't think she's my actual aunt, walk up carrying two heavy baskets. More food! Even the skeletal detective is afraid of eating by this point, so he slaps shut his notebook, bows, and tells Bà good-bye. He's leaving, for real. So that's what it takes to chase him out of here! Go do your job, go do your job, I sing to myself. With the detective gone, half the noises disappear.

The two guests sit down and stare. This happens a lot, maybe-relatives stopping by to watch me eat. Do they want to make sure I don't throw out their food? Do they want to see what gets stuck in my braces? On display, with Bà monitoring me, I do my part and chew.

When I'm done with my soup I don't look up, so afraid they'll open the baskets. But they seem preoccupied. Yes!

"Miss, Cô Tâm has requested my services to extend to you her invitation to a special gatherin' that happens monthly. You probably have been informed that our village is known for its delicate, exquisite embroidery, a skill passed from mothers to daughters and guarded from strangers. Cô Tâm will be teachin' a basic yet crucial stitch today and invites you to participate."

My instant reaction is, of course, no, as in NO. I blank out my face, using my little trick of mentally staring into an empty gray box. I hate how my fingers cramp up while clutching a slippery needle that would prick me and leave tiny beads of blood.

But what's a bit of blood when I can break from the numbing cycle of eating and sleeping? And I think Út said there's internet connection in her house. I need to send Mom a long email about the detective. How hard can it be to lure the guard here? Mom should take over.

All right, I'll confess, it's not about Mom at all. I really want to check FB. Talking to Montana is too heart-attacky, but on FB I won't have to fake my voice to sound unannoyed and interested.

I jump up, saying embroidery has been passed down to me too. Mom made sure I knew how to sew, embroider, stitch a tent, hunt for wild mushrooms, detect edible wild greens, strain drinking water out of mud, resole shoes using old tires. I have no idea why I would need to know all that growing up in Laguna, but I rarely win with Contradictory Momma. She says the key to life is to be prepared for the worst . . . while wearing white and perfecting your complexion, of course.

I bow to my maybe-aunt. I'm so agreeable I shock myself.

Bà doesn't join us for embroidery because of her weak eyes. She's probably happier being alone and chanting for Ông. These days her chants can last an afternoon and must be whispered to save her throat. Way back she taught me *"Nam Mô A Di Đà Phật, Nam Mô Quan Thế Âm Bồ Tát,"* when other kids were learning "Twinkle Twinkle Little Star." There weren't hand motions in my lullaby, which was actually an ancient Buddhist sutra in Sanskrit (how worldly was I?), but whispering those words always sank me toward sleep.

CHAPTER 13

At least twenty girls are at Út's two-story house, built of the same stacked-rectangle design. Is there one architect for the whole country? The girls are all wearing loose pants and matching blouses that could be pajamas. Such intricate embroideries! After that much work, the girls should show them off, pajamas or not.

They giggle and hide their mouths behind cupped hands as soon as I walk in. On display again, for once not while eating, I hope I remember not to pick my nose or, even worse, scrape gunk from my teeth and smell it. Private habit of mine, which no one would know about if I had my own room. But in this land of togetherness; wanting my own space, even for a little while, equates to wanting to go to jail.

On a round table sits a huge piece of white silk, sketched in pencil with willow trees around a pond where girls in cone hats are paddling little boats. Square huts stand in the background. Where is this? I haven't seen any huts in Vietnam. It's the kind of scene tourists take home.

Five girls sit at this table. The rest scatter around tables in the back, each with her own piece of white cloth, smaller and not silk. I don't see a computer in this room. How do I poke around?

Cô Tâm stands. *"Today we will practice the caterpillar crawl, a forward stitch that must be done precisely to show absolutely no discrepancy between the front and back sides. Spacing must be tiny as a third of a rice grain to camouflage each puncture. Make certain your puncture points follow in step, much like matching someone's footsteps, to create the illusion of an uninterrupted line."*

Huh? The girls at the front table are obviously pros and each start on a willow branch. Seamless. I begin mine, thin brown thread attached to a thin thin needle. Just a straight line. No big deal. I go in and out, in and out. Mom will be thrilled to know she's passed on a skill still in vogue. How useful though, I can't say.

Suddenly, my right palm is slapped.

"Not acceptable." Cô Tâm tut-tuts me. *"Take it out and begin again."*

Anh Minh, not self-conscious at all from being the only boy here, whispers the translation, as if anyone, Vietnamese speaking or not, would ever misunderstand a tut-tut. Fine, I take out the stitch. I wonder if there's ever been a nonscholarly village boy who wants to embroider or an ocean-loving village girl who would rather raise shrimps.

Út might be that girl. She sits a few tables to my right and just got her hand slapped too. Her thread is knotted and can't be pulled through. At least I'm not that bad. Her mother has to clip, cut out the tangles, reknot the thread, and hand back the needle. Út looks so miserable I almost feel sorry for her. For once, I don't see Froggy or the basket.

Slap. Ooowww. Who knew such a sweet-looking woman could be so aggressive? Cô Tâm would never make it in Laguna, where parents count to twenty to let pass the urge to raise their voices ever so slightly to their kids. Admittedly, these same kids should be screamed at, they're so obnoxious and demanding. I'm not obnoxious or demanding. Right?

I have to take my stitches out again. Other slaps ring out across the room. Only Út and I wrinkle our brows in annoyance. The others concentrate like they're putting together a five-thousand-piece puzzle. I force my brow to smooth out, remembering that I need Cô Tâm's permission to use their computer, probably kept upstairs.

"Do girls learn to embroider over there?" I hear the question and the translation but I'm so intent on getting each stitch perfectly spaced I don't get that someone just spoke to me. Anh Minh has to shake my shoulder a little.

All are staring at me. They've stopped stitching, so I stop. It feels really good to relax my eyes and stretch my fingers. If I answer the truth, a quick no, then I'd have to go right back to stitching. So . . .

"They don't embroider as much as, uhmm, add things onto their stuff because I guess it's very important for each girl to wear her own design so that her personality shows through."

After the translation, all faces stare blankly. Might as well give Anh Minh something to do and so I keep going. "Over there you can't stand out unless you're different and that says you have the confidence to be creative and wear whatever you think is unique. Yes, that's it, it's a very big deal to be unique because the goal is to be an individual and pursue your own vision."

Anh Minh signals for me to pause so he can get all that out. No one has to sew while I talk or am being translated. Cool. Word stretching is not a problem. I haven't suffered through the detective for nothing.

Út's sister, Chị Lan, speaks. Her voice, which I'm hearing for the first time, is as clear and pretty as she is. Anh Minh stands taller while translating for her. "If everyone is unique, how can one stand out?"

"I guess then you'd have to be superunique, like beyond the beyond. If everyone is dyeing their shoelaces to represent their true selves, pink for romantic, baby blue for innocent, fuchsia for independent, raspberry for countercultural, then maybe you'd paint your shoes or attach buttons or glue on beads to stand out."

Út just has to butt in. Translation: "Who decides pink is for stomach-coiling feelings and fuchsia for self-freedom? If everyone agrees on the meanings of those colors, how is that unique?" She sits there rubbing her buzz cut like it's a fashion statement. Oh, she's so annoying.

I blind her with my braces. "You're unique when you're the first one to do something unique."

Anh Minh barely has my comeback translated when Út already has her mouth open. "How can you possibly know if you are the first one? At your school? In the world? No one is unique if everyone is tryin' to be unique. If a male frog is croakin' a special pattern to attract a female, the act itself is mundane because every male frog has a song but its pattern is particular to that frog. Yet it is rather impossible to ascertain that no other frog anywhere else has tried the exact pattern."

Bet you she's the type to raise her hand in class and everyone groans.

I'm not backing down. "When my friend Montana wore a thong to class the first day of sixth grade, everyone thought she was unique and started copying her. Not just our grade, but the whole school, then everywhere. I'm not kidding, everybody wears them in America."

Okay, not even close to everyone, especially not me, but who would know here? I can say anything about life in America and they'd believe me. I've appointed myself an expert on America.

Many are asking, *"What did she say?"* I understand but have to look blank. This clandestine double-language trick is exhausting.

Anh Minh seems panicky. "Miss, are you talkin' about the truly revealin' undergarment of ladies? I don't know if there's a Vietnamese name for it."

I try to help. "Could you ask Cô Tâm for a pair of panties?"

Anh Minh turns red. He whispers to Cô Tâm and then just leaves. Walks straight out of the house. Hey, can an official, personal translator just blow off his duties? Not professional at all! Fine, I'll do everything myself. I pull down my capris just a bit to show the top of my panties. *"Có không?"* Have this?

Cô Tâm, looking worried, comes back with a pair: white, big, grade school.

I hold up a pair of scissors and ask with my eyes if it's okay to cut. Still looking worried, she nods. I must say the Vietnamese are the best hosts in the world. They just want to please you, even if it means ruining obviously brand-new underwear.

I cut two half circles from the cheek-covering part, leaving the unmistakable tree shape of a thong. Then I hem each side. Not even close to perfect stitches, but good enough. I hold it up, ta-da. Massive confusion. Making a point is such work. I'm going to have to do it . . . put on the thong outside my capris to show how it works. The girls just shake their heads.

"They wear tiny underwear on the outside? Is that unique?"

"Why can't the buttocks be covered?"

"Is this like that yellow-haired singer wearing a bra shaped like two miniature cone hats?"

Ugh, I go in the back and put on the thong under my capris. I come out and pull my pants in tight and point to my butt. *"Không thấy,"* can't see. They gather around.

"Can't see what?" Út says.

"Cái lằn," the lines, I almost scream. I spin her around, pull tight her icky man shorts and point to the panty lines. "Yes." I point to her butt. "No." I point to mine.

"Why can't we have lines?" Út again.

I answer, *"Không sạch,"* not clean. I mean not clean lines, as in you'd want smooth, sleek slopes down your butt cheeks, but my speaking skills only go so far.

Cô Tâm understands. *"Đúng, sạch hơn,"* yes, it is cleaner. *"Con hiểu tiếng Việt phải không?"* You understand Vietnamese, don't you?

Did I just give my secret away, over a thong? Noooo, I was waiting to reveal my listening skills, imagining some dramatic scene that would embarrass Út, the ultrapain, like telling everyone that Froggy is actually a toad or, hmmm, what else would annoy a girl who's forever rubbing her buzz and grinning?

I panic and lie. *"Không,"* no. Not really a lie because speaking at a Tarzan level doesn't actually count as speaking.

Cô Tâm looks confused, trying to process that I understand enough to answer I don't understand. She smiles and pats me on the head anyway. Told you, perfect host.

I did it; I got to the mom. She loves me. I point to her mismatched, frumpy, froggy-obsessed daughter. *"Làm?"* Make? Meaning make a thong for Út?

Her mother nods and runs off. I can feel Út's stare searing through my skull, but I still look straight at her and smile, huge and metal. Cô Tâm comes back with not one pair, but an armful. Each girl begins cutting. The afternoon should pass quickly for me, not so much for you-know-who.

There's no computer. A whole afternoon spent gnarling my fingers and going blind—for nothing. Add to that the awful truth that I've forced a whole group of clean, trusting girls to become self-conscious about lines on their butt cheeks. Each girl is wearing her new thong. Some have embroidered chrysanthemums or orchids around the hems. They took the project way too seriously.

We're leaving now to go eat *phở*, in celebration of our creations. I started this mess so I have to come along.

On the main dirt path to the open market, we begin picking at our cracks, straighten up, then pick again. I can't believe I got myself into this. I hate thongs. I hate how they look, how they feel, what they represent. Never have I worn something so tight as to need a thong. But I can't backtrack now. They think I'm an expert on American girly cleanliness.

I'm making it a point to walk behind Út, who's really slow. She doesn't just pick but scratches, wiggles, lifts a leg, and writhes in obvious misery. This is so worth my own suffering. I don't see how Montana wears them every day. Come to think of it, she did spend most of the time picking at her booty.

Because Út and I lag behind, we're the only two to see her sister's best friend, Chị Ngọc, come out of nowhere in a . . . fluffy light-pink skirt! I have to address Lan and Ngọc as Chị to show, you guessed it, r-e-s-p-e-c-t. Just a while ago, Chị Ngọc was wearing flowy silk pants like everyone else. How did she change so fast? She doesn't see us. Without saying a word, Út and I hide behind dusty leafy bushes on opposite sides of the dirt path.

Chị Ngọc keeps glancing back as if waiting for someone. It can't be for her best friend, who is way ahead with the group. I hear stomping. Anh Minh comes running up the path, panting, stirring the red dust. I almost sneeze but catch myself just in time. Why is he running? Where did he go after walking out? He's really panicking.

Chị Ngọc stops. Is she smirking? I know that smirk, all eerie like Montana's.

"Where is Lan?" Anh Minh asks. *"I must inform her I have to leave now."* Anh Minh is sweating and inhaling gulps of dust.

Where's he going? I'm about to jump out when Chị Ngọc flips her hair. Please, the predictable hair flip. She's talking to him in a baby voice, all the while tilting her head and twisting a strand of hair around her index finger. Has she been watching bad Hollywood teen movies? Or did the American teen movies copy Asian flirty moves that probably have been around from way back when?

He runs away. Hey, I almost yell, but Chị Ngọc calls out his name in a helpless voice, forcing him to turn around.

She turns and flips up her skirt, exposing two white moons separated by the silky tree trunk. The moons bounce a little. NOOOO!!! I can see Út's eyeballs about to booong out of their sockets. Anh Minh chokes, stumbles, then runs even faster. Chị

Ngọc (should I keep calling her Chị?) fluffs down her skirt and prances along. I notice her heels, not Hollywood heels, but in this land of flip-flops, heels!

I look over at Út. We blink, no doubt trying to wash away the image of white, bouncy moons. Both our faces scrunch up, then we look at each other, really look at each other, and crack up, braces glinting in the sun.

CHAPTER 14

Anh Minh has been called to the American embassy in Hanoi, this much everyone knows. His parents, who have sold their home and moved in with his aunt and maternal grandparents so all can pitch in to cover what his scholarship doesn't, talked about their son to his aunt's cousin. That cousin told someone, who told Cô Hạnh, who acts as the village newspaper.

Now during meals/chewing events, villagers come by to ask Bà if I, being American born, have some magic dust that can poof away their darling's student visa problems. I wish. If I were so embassy-connected, I'd be home already, parental approval or not.

With Anh Minh gone, Út and I are the only two to have witnessed the moon flashing. Somehow, this unites us. Without actually speaking or even a handshake, we have decided to take down Con Ngọc. BTW, I no longer have to say Chị Ngọc. Út has downgraded her all the way to Con. It doesn't sound like much, but that's the equivalent of saying "Yo, Ngọc."

I'm not even sure what I have against Con Ngọc. I could get righteous and say it's about taking a stance against deception. But really, Con Ngọc cannot be the first person to use her butt cheeks to maneuver feelings to her advantage. Not classy, but it happens. Or I could say I'm helping out true love, but then true love wouldn't fall for a moon-flashing trick anyway. Fine, I admit I'm all hyper about Con Ngọc because I have nothing else to do.

Hours here stretch into days and those days disappear into routines and before I know it, I'm hanging out with Út. I wouldn't say she's fun but definitely different. I'm so desperate for company I would pass time with Froggy. It's a bonus that Út comes along.

Besides, focusing on the village triangle keeps me from obsessing about being stuck in this village. If things turn out well here, then the good karma might carry all the way back to Laguna. I know that sounds desperate, but you try being banished to a swampy sauna and not succumb to a little superstition. Did I just release an SAT alert? *Succumb*. It's a great word. I no longer have the energy to monitor myself. Tap into whatever vocabulary vault you want, brain, I'm just trying to hang on until Anh Minh returns or the detective returns or my life returns.

I wonder what's keeping the detective from dragging in the

overly sensitive guard. Really, who cares if anyone thinks Bà is paying him for information? Doesn't he want to be paid? I've not voiced this out loud because I'm being sensitive.

Dad, still, is waiting to see if his patient will recover. Something about a mom letting her toddler eat real rice instead of *cháo* too soon after the surgery and now the palate has healed with grains of rice stuck inside the roof of the mouth. Mom has hired scouts to hike into the mountains, get updates, then hike back to where there's Wi-Fi to send her reports. She can arrange that, but she's as helpless as we all are in getting the guard to appear.

Thank goodness for the fourteen-hour time difference because one of us is always sleepy, so our texts are short. I text that I'm hanging in there (sort of), that I'm eating well (too well), that I'm helping Bà (who's in easy, quiet mode), that I'm staying busy (plotting a love story, not the most brilliant way to spend time, but I don't have many choices), that I miss her dearly (which causes an avalanche of smiley faces in reply). My final text always uses the SAT word for the day in a sentence, which is also the signal for my brain to forget the word.

My mind is supercooperative these days. I've willed it to put Montana and HIM on pause. I had no idea I was so powerful, but so far, I've only panicked three times. I've got a bet going with myself. If Anh Minh and Chị Lan do get together, I'll initiate a real conversation with HIM when I get home. Any other ending, I'll have to think about letting HIM go. Not that HE was ever mine, but HE has been ultrareal in my mind.

***

We know where Anh Minh is, we can guess what he's wearing (blue pants/white shirt, the self-imposed uniform of any boy here who opens a book), we also have detailed reports on what he's eating (phone calls from maybe-relatives in Hanoi).

But no one knows when he's coming back. It's been four long days.

Anh Minh doesn't have a cell phone. Út, subbing as my translator, is determined to email him. That's why she needs me. It's okay for me to email my official translator, but what reason would Út have? Appearances, proper, improper, the rules are endless.

Turns out, Út has been studying English since first grade. She likes to memorize grammar books. No comment. So she's reading fluently in English, but when it comes to speaking, I can't understand one word she says. Her Vietnamese-born English teacher studied French first and thinks it's classy to pronounce everything with a French accent. *Conversation* turns into "con-va-SA-see-ong," and *iodine* becomes "ee-OR-dean," which came up in a panicky moment when Froggy hurt his leg. But that's another story.

Even without understanding her English, I get Út because she talks to herself in Vietnamese, like a lot. It's not my fault I have the superpower to hear Vietnamese. Út keeps mumbling, *"He has the luck to be in Hà Nội. One trip there, that's all I need, one trip."*

What's so great about that moped-insane, horn-obsessed, body-congested, nostril-bruising city?

Út, though, is a remarkable speller with perfect handwriting. So, as long as she writes things down, I get it, although it's still fastest when she talks to herself.

She writes, "We need Anh Minh to confess to sister. His feelings and her feelings are truth."

I write back in English but Út can't read it. Mom always nagged me about my scribbles while I argued we have technology for a reason. Who knew I'd be across the world scratching on paper with a stubby pencil?

Now I talk and Út writes. But I have to speak Tarzan-ish Vietnamese because Út says she doesn't understand my non-Frenchy English. It's exhausting, but so is my life.

"Làm gì?" What to do?

Perfect cursive: "Anh Minh and my sister must stare at each other alone."

"Làm sao?" How? *"Đi rồi."* He's gone.

"We will email that you require him."

"Cho gì?" For what?

Út frowns, staring me down like I'm useless and she has to think of everything. I smile sweetly. It feels weird, all this effort to be charming, but life would be unbearable if she and my translator were to disappear.

"No, tell better your Bà needs him here. Now."

"Cho gì?" For what?

She gives me another exasperated look. Fine, think, think, brain, think.

CHAPTER 15

Before lunch the next day, our scheming takes us to the stacked house where everyone first greeted me and Bà. Red of blood, yellow of skin, five stories. You can't miss it. The woman who answers has the smoothest, clearest skin I've ever seen. Mom, who spends half her paychecks on jars of face cream, would be so jealous. She's Cô Hạnh, Út's real aunt and I'm sure my maybe-one.

"Ah, Út, right on time, I need you to pick rau muống*. And you, come in and sit."*

Apparently, you can't show up to someone's house with internet service and zoom straight to the computer. First, Út asks after Cô Hạnh's husband, son, daughter, mother, father, countless cousins, barking dog, algae in the pond, some ripening fruit at Chú Tư's (*chú* means uncle, another maybe-relative?).

We all head to the back to look at the fruit. I've yet to meet anyone in the village who doesn't go gaga for fruit and vegetables. I could put this backyard scene on a postcard—it's that dreamy. Wooden houses surround a huge pond. Each house has a porch that juts out into the water and sits on stilts. Gigantic orange koi swim under the porch planks. Willows are planted like fences so you can kinda see your neighbors, but not really.

Út points to the tree across the pond that has branches crawling out just above the water. So cool. Red clumps cling to the branches. *"Are they ripe yet?"*

"I wouldn't know. You know Chú Tư cherishes them as if they're his children. I'm lucky if I get one at the end of the season."

"He's always given quả sung *to me. He likes me."* When Út says something like that, she's just stating the truth. He probably thinks she's great. I've noticed people either swoon or sneer at her. My sneering is moving toward the middle.

Suddenly, Cô Hạnh grabs me by the chin. Her eyes bug out and zoom in. Forget about swooning over me, she's even past sneering, she's downright horrified.

"Tut-tut, what have you been putting on your skin?"

Nothing! Honest! I'm not into makeup. Watching Montana apply rounds and rounds of lip gloss has damaged my view of what is probably a perfectly normal activity. I try to wrestle away but Cô Hạnh grips my chin.

"What's clogging your pores? We have to cure these pimples before they leave scars."

PIMPLES? SCARS!!! I just realized I haven't seen a mirror in forever, since the hotel. And I haven't missed it! That's because I've been living in shock.

How can I have pimples? I've been so careful, washing my face with a cloth twice a day and never touching my fingers to my . . . OMG, I have PIMPLES! I thought my face was a little bumpy when I applied sunblock every day, but without a mirror I just imagined I had a heat rash or insect bites or some other consequence of living in muggy land.

"Gương!" Mirror! Cô Hạnh leads me to a huge mirror with lightbulbs all around like you'd see in a movie star's dressing room. The megawatts don't hide one little bump. Tons of yellow dots are pushing up on tiny red hills scattered all over my forehead and cheeks. The colors of Vietnam's flag. ON MY FACE! This is not how I imagined connecting with my roots.

"Không sao, không sao," not a problem, not a problem, Cô Hạnh murmurs, seeing me close to tears. *"I know exactly how to cure this."*

It's fascinating that people will talk to me like I understand, even though I'm playing dumb. I think people just like to listen to their voices.

First, Cô Hạnh sends Út to the kitchen to bring back a bowl of raw rice soaked in warm water and citrus peels. I swear Út is kinda smirking. Whatever, deep breath, deep breath.

Cô Hạnh then goes to the garden and picks lots of leaves and a cucumber. Is the cure a salad? Right away I start panicking about the right dressing because I can only eat salads with this one balsamic vinaigrette. Without it, I'll gag and that always makes my stomach . . . Focus, focus! I sit on my hands and make myself look away from the brightest mirror on earth to prevent an urge to pick and squeeze.

Út returns first. Patting her own cheek, which I admit is smooth and clear but I bet little cancer cells are blooming beneath all that bronzeness, Út writes, "Go in the sun and clean your skin."

"No!"

Út shrugs. Look at her, all buzzy and bronzed and bracy and mismatched and frumpy, but she's as happy as she can be. How is that possible?

Cô Hạnh comes back with handfuls of leaves and asks Út to wash them and bring the pestle and mortar set. Út sighs and yawns. Obviously, she does not share our urgency.

Meanwhile, Cô Hạnh strains the rice water and tells me to splash my face, after tying back my hair and tut-tutting that it should always be off my forehead. The water smells of steamed rice and clementines, like Bà's room. In tiny pats with a cloth, Cô Hạnh dries my face, where the skin somehow feels tighter, and puts a magnifying glass to it. *"What's the white sticky lotion on it?"*

I pull from my pants a tube of Mom's sunblock. For as long as I can remember, Mom has bought me clothes with pockets big enough to carry a tube. Cô Hạnh squeezes a little between her fingers, mashes it, then more tut-tuts. *"Like putting glue to your skin, your pores can't breathe, not in this humid corner of the world."*

I stand there. She'll keep talking. *"Better to block with cloth and spare your skin from chemicals."*

I have to wash my face again, scrubbing lightly with this really soft, warm cloth smelling of grapefruit blossoms. Not a spa treatment, but not bad at all.

Út appears just as Cô Hạnh pulls something out of her own pocket. She heads straight for Út, who starts backing away. I don't blame her. Cô Hạnh, abnormally fast, hooks something behind Út's ears. It's a flowery cloth mask that starts below the eyes and goes way past the neck, getting tucked inside the collar of Út's ratty shirt. Not done, Cô Hạnh adds a floppy hat lined with the same glaring cloth.

"Wear them," she admonishes. *"In the South, everyone is wearing face masks. But mine covers all the way down your neck. Much better, especially with a hat. These are going to sell well."*

Neither Út nor I look convinced. But if enduring a facial and wearing a ninja mask will lead us to the internet, then we're in. But then, mask and hat on, Út has to go out back and get into a canoe and paddle around the pond to pick deep green floating leafy stalks called *rau muống*. Út doesn't even fight back. This from a girl who has a smart comeback for just about every situation? So much more is at stake than the internet. What has Cô Hạnh got on her?

Back inside, Cô Hạnh is grinding leaves and powder and ginger into a paste. I know all about ginger root, Bà's favorite cure-all after Tiger Balm. Bà nibbles on a fresh, fiery stub to rid herself of nausea, dizziness, cramps, aches, a bad taste on her tongue . . . you get the idea.

Cô Hạnh signals for me to sit in this tilted chair by the window. I'm staring at the ceiling. Then she actually scoops out a green, gooey paste and smears it, ever so gently, all over my face. It smells like mint plus ginger plus decaying organic matter, so basically fancy compost. I breathe through my mouth. I know all about compost—one of Mom's many obsessions. You throw one apple core away in my house and you'll be digging in the trash, then taking a trip to the backyard compost bin.

From the left corner, I can kinda see the computer calling me, green light on. The torments a girl has to endure in Vietnam to send one lousy email! Deal with it, I tell myself. Bà says everybody suffers from something at some point. It's apparently my turn. When down, Bà says, try to imagine a rosier future. How about if Anh Minh would please reappear, I promise to prioritize his drama by playing matchmaker. Then the universe will register my kindness score and bring the guard to Bà. Once she accepts Ông is gone, we will surely be going home.

The more I think about how long it takes to find acceptance, the more scared I am. How long does acceptance take? It's been decades and Bà's not there yet. I have to block the thought or I'll start sweating under the herbal mask and who knows how Cô Hạnh will react?

I can kinda see Út hunched over in the canoe, picking picking, stopping often to push back the floppy hat. Shocking that she hasn't flung it into the pond.

After the mask dries, we wash it off with more rice water. Wow, the yellow bumps have been sucked out of me, leaving little pink hills. Cô Hạnh grins as if saying, I'm that good. She puts thin cucumber slices all over my face. In the canoe, Út is hunched way over, about to fall in, talking to something in the water. Weird for anyone else, but for Út . . . not so much.

"Don't use the white paste anymore," Cô Hạnh says. *"This company came over and gave away free tubes and after one usage everyone threw them in the trash heap. Skin does not like chemicals, which will enlarge your pores to resemble dots on a grapefruit peel. A cloth mask lets your pores breathe. I will make one as a present for you. What color?"*

I've never been so self-conscious about my pores. Maybe I should cover mine behind a mask and be done. As for the mask color, no need to respond. Cô Hạnh will answer her own question.

"Đỏ? *Yes, I have the perfect red cloth."*

Út comes in just as Cô Hạnh removes my cucumber slices. The hills are flat with a hint of pink. Amazing. Cô Hạnh taps a watery lotion on me. *"Don't touch,"* she warns.

Út leans in for a closer look. *"You won't scar."*

That's the nicest thing she's ever said to me.

Finally, after mashing up more leaves for me to take home (yippie), after eating a mound of *rau muống* sautéed in garlic to cleanse our liver thus our skin, after slurping scorching lotus tea in the middle of a hot afternoon to harmonize body and air temperatures, after soaking our feet in jasmine water for I don't know why, after listening to Cô Hạnh talk about how pretty she used to be (apparently it's fine to compliment yourself here, as I've heard countless other maybe-aunts gush about their youthful beauty), Út and I are led to the holy computer. If I ever make it back to my very own PC, I shall kiss it once in the morning and once at night.

While my phone charges, I open emails from Mom with taglines like "urgent" and "near death with worries." Mom loves melodrama. We've been texting and she's cranky with worries about her court case yet she still has time to write. Answer: "don't worry, please, i'm actually doing really great. you're right; village life is so fascinating. i'm learning so much. the internet here is mercurial and could shut down any minute. love you 100,000 times to the moon and back, mai mai."

I might have slapped on too much mush, but Mom will love it and back off. Notice I did not type anything about going home. Mom knows I want to, so I'll be mature and leave it at that. Besides, that ultimate wish isn't happening, at all. Notice my strategic use of an SAT word and my childhood sign-off that has always melted Mom. We should be good for a while. We probably won't even need to text.

The emails from Montana I delete without opening. Better not to know. I immediately regret it and retrieve one from the trash. It reads, "should i trim my hair half or one inch?" In Laguna, I would have indulged her and answered with a straight face, but across the world, DELETE. We haven't talked or texted since that one call and, weird, but I don't really miss her.

As Út and I planned, I compose an email to Anh Minh, who already emailed me a while back so we can be FFL. He actually knows some slang.

ANH MINH,

BÀ IS IN DIRE NEED OF YOUR ASSISTANCE. SHE IS IN PAIN. I DON'T KNOW WHAT TO DO. YOU ARE THE ONLY ONE WE CAN RELY ON.

PLEASE HURRY,
Mai/Mia

I learned melodrama from the best source: Mom. Út nudges me out of the way. She adds, with equal urgency:

ĐI RA HỒ HOÀN KIẾM BAN TỐI. RẤT CẦN. CÓ THẤY ÁNH SÁNG TRONG NƯỚC KHÔNG? Út

How did she add those little marks in an email? I bet those are the exact ones Anh Minh would love to cram in my already saturated brain. Maybe he doesn't need to come back all that soon. Just kidding. I need drama, intrigue, something to cheer for while I'm on the longest wait ever for the most stubborn guard ever.

Út can barely stand still she's so happy. I don't bother to ask.

From the way her eyes sparkle, I'm guessing it's devious. Poor Con Ngọc, she has no idea what she's up against.

Then, because I can't help it, I click into FB. Mistake! On my wall, in color-popping photos, is Montana with her towel around HIS waist, trying to get HIM to dance. She's bent over, boobs spilling, butt bow wiggling.

I flick off the screen. Not fast enough. All around me are maybe-relatives, where did they come from? Of course, not quiet maybe-relatives, that's like asking for world peace. Instead, I get the ones with amplified tut-tuts. They let loose all sorts of comments, but I'm so hot and heart-poundy I can't really understand. I sit still and let exclamations singsong around me. No doubt this will take a while, as anyone who first sees Montana and her butt bow will have much to say.

I look over at Út. A slight downward curve of her mouth. I get exactly what she's thinking: we should have gone back to the hot shack/internet café. Not once have I imagined I would be wishing for a DIAL-UP. But I am. In that suffocating shack, at least I would have this thing from memory called privacy.

CHAPTER 16

After my email in bold and all caps, you'd think Anh Minh would come running, pleading for forgiveness. But nothing. Maybe he went back to school in Houston. But it's still early in the summer.

I'm awake, waiting for Út. It's so early even the rooster is still snoozing. Út will come by any minute now, like she has the last three dawns, so we can make tea.

The morning after Anh Minh left, Cô Tâm and Cô Hạnh, sisters who I've learned are our meal providers, came by after breakfast to have tea with Bà. One sip of the lukewarm tea left at dawn and they just about spat. Tea should be freshly brewed, they chimed, not sitting all morning and turning dark and bitter. It tasted fine to me. But I've learned I know nothing about tea, herbs, rice, vegetables, fruit, and all protein sources. For example, you must not eat shrimps unless you've witnessed them jumping at the market. Frozen shrimps are for the undiscriminating foreign market; dead shrimps along with heads and shells become fertilizer. At least I will never be expected to shop or cook while we're here.

Making tea, though, should be teachable, even to me. It was decided Út and I would make the first pot at dawn, with other girls coming by at midmorning, midafternoon, and twilight. Probably the whole village is waiting for evidence that I can do something other than eat and sleep, which I must say I've accomplished with grace. I don't chomp like helicopter blades or slurp like a dog or sip like a wind tunnel and I never snore. Impressive, right?

Every task takes planning at Ông's Brother's old house. To get a cup of tea to Bà by sunrise, I must get up an hour before. Út has been waking me by shaking my big toe, still inside the mosquito net with the rest of me.

There's her shadow now, alert and focused. Of course, she would be a morning person. She comes closer, closer, reaches for my right big toe.

"RAH," I pounce and roar/whisper because Bà's asleep in the net.

Út just stares at me. Could she at least jump and play along with my sad attempt to pump some fun, spontaneity, surprise back into my life? No, I guess not. Her shadow looks bored. Fine, I crawl out in flowy pajamas and socks, not at all ready to work but not wanting the whole village to think I'm that lazy. A little lazy I can live with, but not to the point of embarrassment to Bà.

All cooking is done on the back porch, under a tin canopy that blocks the constant rain. Out here, we're next to the rain barrel and do not have to lug water into the house that doesn't have indoor plumbing. It does have electricity, although it doesn't have any outlets so I keep charging the phone at Út's house.

For decades, Ông's Brother has prepared meals out here on a three-prong clay "stove" that sits right in the middle of the cement porch. Maybe not the exact same stove, but I have a feeling the same design has been around since people discovered clay. The stove, shaped like a big pot with three feet, has a bottom made of mesh wires where the fire is built. A pot or kettle sits on a rack on top of the stove and somehow things actually cook.

To do anything with the stove, I have to squat, which is murder on untrained thighs. Of course Bà does not have stove duty. I wonder what Ông's Brother has against a bench and a stool.

"Do by self today," Út writes. Predawn and she's ready with a pad and pencil. Út, ever efficient, knows how to fire charcoal even though her home has an inside kitchen with electric burners. Not the safest invention, but I love how the rings turn rosy-ready with a twist of a knob.

No such luck with the antiquated, cold, blackened clay block in front of me. I shake my head to mean I'm not ready for a solo shot at firing charcoal. I can't speak yet, too early to chase down the few Vietnamese words I know and mold them into a broken phrase. I'm a twilight person.

Bossy Út wrinkles her brows and points at the soot-encrusted, misshapen kettle. She can still be so annoying.

I take the kettle to the lidded rain barrel, fill it three-quarters full—too much and water will spurt out while boiling, too little and some amount of coal and effort will be wasted. At least I've mastered pouring water into the kettle, after many sighs from Út.

Back to the stove, I set the kettle aside, squat down. Oh, my thighs. Út hands me newspaper strips for the bottommost layer. Then I add in order: straw, bark, and finally three precious charcoal briquettes. I've never seen anyone here use more than three. Light a match, orange/red flames spread to the newspaper.

"Bend down," Út writes. It's always like this with bossy Út.

She hands me a rattan fan. "Just enough," she adds. Too much fanning and the flame will extinguish, too little and it will just smoke. That has happened before, again causing many sighs. This time I'm the world's best waver of the handheld fan. The fire catches and soon the briquettes start to get rosy on the bottom like three baboons with red bottoms. Bà told me a folktale about why the baboons ended up with flaming rears, though I forget.

"Careful, do not waste." Út taps her pencil for emphasis.

I know, I want to snap. The trick is to put the kettle to boil before the briquettes are fully red, as to not waste heat, then you have to throw ash on the briquettes just before the water reaches full boiling point, as to not waste heat, because the water will keep boiling while the charcoal cools down.

"Do not waste," Út writes, and taps. I get it, already. This is something every villager says at least a hundred times a day. Don't waste the vegetable-washing water, splash it on the grapefruit tree instead. Of course it's the rainy season and everything is plenty dewy and damp, including me, but why argue? Don't waste anything made of glass or plastic because glass and plastic can be reused ad nauseam. Don't waste anything resembling food because the chickens or pigs or water buffaloes or roaming dogs will want it. Don't waste . . . a string for retying, a rubber band for conquering dry noodles or hair, rice bags for dishcloths, fish bones for fertilizer, chicken bones to be cooked down to mush for dogs, feathers for pillows. Anything that comes out of the earth must be returned to the earth. Mom would be in recycling heaven here.

Over and over I hear, *"If everyone uses more than their share, how can the earth support us?"* Someone should paint that on a sign at the village entrance to warn visitors.

The water boils just as the briquettes cool to gray, the remaining clumps saved, no doubt, for another teaching moment.

Út beams at me. Against my will, I'm very proud.

At sunrise, we grin until our cheeks hurt while presenting Bà and Ông's Brother with a perfectly steeped pot of lotus tea. My only chore done, I have fifteen hours left until bedtime. If Út weren't around, I'd be pulling out my hair and making wigs for tiny invisible dolls. Who knew Út would become so useful? Being with her keeps me from analyzing the four words HE said especially to me.

Yes, I know, HE is supposed to be on pause.

Út finds remarkable ways to waste time. All day, I follow her around and she actually lets me, even during nap time when we watch Froggy nap in Cô Hạnh's pond. It's as boring as it sounds, but I take what I can get. We don't even talk/write that much. Fine by me. Our days run together into a long stream of a few chores, then lots of sitting around. Not much happens, but then everything happens.

While the elders sip tea (I hope they fully comprehend what the vapors rising from their cozy cups cost me in sleep and energy), Út and I go to her house. I change out of Bà's pajamas into a flowy silk outfit borrowed from Út's sister. I text Mom a picture and she asks if my matching set is day wear. If she can't tell, why would it matter?

Apparently, Út doesn't own anything but dusty pants and ratty T-shirts. The new me no longer judges.

Aside from having electrical outlets and an indoor kitchen, Út's house also has the loveliest of all modern inventions: an indoor bathroom. At Ông's Brother's house, there's this flimsy outback wooden shed, where you squat over a hole that connects to somewhere, and after you've done your business you splash everything down with exactly one bucket of water. I've gotten used to that. The new me astonishes even me.

Út's bathroom not only has a toilet but also a shiny faucet, which I must not turn on. That task belongs to an adult. The faucet fills a barrel, from where water is portioned out with a scoop made from a hard, halved squash shell fitted with a bamboo handle. When I say everything is recycled here, I mean everything. I pour the water into a cup, but only half full. That's all I get to brush teeth, just enough to rinse once and wash out my brush. Bà learned her half-a-cup-tooth-brushing habit here.

Cô Hạnh happens to be at Út's house and treats—or forces—everyone through a mini herbal-goop facial, followed by a steamed towel that has been boiled in citrus water. At least the last part is spa-ish. She grabs my chin, leans close and announces, "Poreless as peach skin." I can't help but giggle. My pores have never been so immaculate or invisible.

After packing in enough breakfast to last until dinner, although we will surely be fed lunch, Út and I stand resigned while Cô Hạnh traps us in her inventions. The sun, barely rising, does not need blocking, but why argue? I now own a face-to-neck mask and a wide-brim hat. The fabric screams red, glowing charcoal red. Why be a subtle ninja when I can announce Cô Hạnh's sun-blocking technique to the world? Út's set brings to mind a ninja in an exploded garden. We're to wear our contraptions and refer interested buyers to Cô Hạnh. Let me say no one has asked.

On the way to the market, we rip off the hats and masks and breathe air instead of our own stale breath.

CHAPTER 17

The Vietnamese like their food fresh. In addition to jumping shrimps, vegetables must be picked at dawn, fruit must be tree-ripened, chicken or pigs killed before sunrise, eggs gathered while warm. Everything gets bundled into baskets tied to mopeds and sped to the market. Daily, every household shops after breakfast for lunch and dinner. After nap time, picked-over items are sold at half price.

I can just hear Mom scoffing at the idea of daily grocery shopping. How would anyone get anything else done? In Laguna, we shop twice a month. If we run out of something, oh well. That's why I've grown addicted to our local fish taco stand.

Every home, except Ông's Brother's, has a refrigerator. I've peeked and seen only chocolate, kept cool from the misty heat and sitting awkward in all that shelf space. This being the land of perfectly portioned eaters, people nibble on one square per day, if that much. So many good habits in one population are really annoying.

I follow Út as she shops from Cô Hạnh's and Cô Tâm's lists. Without exchanging money, merchants know how much and what items to charge to which account. There's a whole lot of trust going on.

Con Ngọc is sauntering over. She spotted us first, so there's no running away.

"Does Lan know Anh Minh won't be back for another week?"

My heart sinks and for a second I think she's better connected to him than we are. But I look at Út, who stands unfazed. Út nose-puffs. I do it too. Whatever it means, I do feel better.

"Yes," Út lies. *"He's been sending messages daily, sometimes twice a day."*

I like the devious Út.

"Where is he living then?" Con Ngọc asks.

I'm not sure if that constitutes a challenge or a sincere question. She and Út stare each other down. I guess I don't count. Suddenly, they break off and rush in opposite directions. I scramble after Út.

We're now in a hurry. Ninja gear on, we drop off the market items; ninja gear off, we run to yet another two-story stacked-rectangle house. Út pushes me forward.

"House of Anh Minh. You can visit. I and my sister have no reason to be here," Út writes. I feel like I've won some obscure lottery.

Út knocks and hides behind me. My sad Vietnamese brain

is drawing from a reservoir of thirty words to babble something about Bà being sick, any reason at all to be here. I'm so nervous I'm shaking.

The sweetest-looking grandmother answers. She must know me because she breaks into a smile. Relieved, I almost hug her but back off just in time. Vietnamese do not hug. So I bow and smile, bow and smile, robot-like.

"Up close you are even taller, my child. Did you already hear?"

I force myself to not give away my superpower by asking, *"Hear what?"*

The grandmother sees Út but is kind enough to ignore her. Footsteps come to the door and Út and I, clutching hands, open our mouths like baby birds.

"ANH MINH."

Still clutching, Út and I jump up and down even though this much emotion at a boy's front door is surely scandalous.

Anh Minh, as if on cue, frowns.

"Why have you presented yourselves at my family's residence?" he says in English for my benefit. How sweet!

I really lose it and hug him. Now I've done it. Anh Minh jumps back as if splashed with hot water. I don't care, I don't care, he's back.

"Did you get my email? You need to acknowledge your feelings to a certain someone who the whole village knows you're so into," I speak really fast because Út is talking over me, *"Did you frequent Hồ Hoàn Kiếm? Were there glowing dots in the dark?"*

"I'm ninety-nine percent sure her feelings are mutual but you've got to step up, so go, make your move, like, right now," I say, while Út says, *"Did you go in the middle of the night? That's the best time because they're so timid."*

I speak up, "I could go with you, would that help?"

But Út is louder, *"Did you hear them? What did they sound like, could you show me now?"*

Anh Minh steps back inside and shuts the door. Hey, what kind of a reunion is this? Út and I both raise our knuckles but think better of knocking. We are not pushy people, so we do the next logical thing . . . plop down in front of the door and wait for him to come out.

Lots of urgent talking behind the door. I'm feeling hopeful. After all, there's a Vietnamese grandmother behind that door, doing what Vietnamese grandmothers do best—getting their way while smiling and patting.

Út and I listen and wait. We have time and more time.

Anh Minh finally appears, not at all surprised when we pop up to attention. Decked out in crisp, clean, blue pants and a white button-down, he walks. We follow, strapping on ninja gears because it's getting toward sunny late morning, and spies will report back to Cô Hạnh.

"Did the glow spots blink on and off or were they steady?" Út lifts her mask to ask, keeping up with Anh Minh on one side.

I'm right there on the other side, lifting my mask, "Do you know where she is?"

He frowns at Út. *"I have been arranging a most urgent matter, without interest or time to attend to your needs."*

Wow, what's happened to my good-natured translator? But then Út can be so annoying. I've tried to convey that to her, but was she paying attention? Noooo. My approach is much more nuanced, subtle.

"You have to tell her, today. She deserves to know." I say it in a fun, jolly manner, flapping my mask up and down, but he gets even more frowny.

"As for you, miss, I need to discuss a lie with you, but later; I must attend to an urgency."

"What lie?"

Without answering, Anh Minh walks fast, way ahead of us, and we have to run after him.

We follow Anh Minh to Cô Hạnh's house, where bunches of girls are smooshed into the front room and spilling out into the yard. Then he disappears.

I squeeze into the crowd, trying to stay close to Út, who has a look of dread and is slithering toward the back. I have a very bad feeling about the gathering. Somehow Út's mom, Cô Tâm, materializes and grips Út's arm. This same moment, a hand grips me. Cô Hạnh smiles and drags me toward Út. Is a really strong grip a trait among Vietnamese women? PBS never mentioned it. At least we got to remove our hats and masks.

Cô Hạnh hands me over to her sister's grip, goes toward the kitchen, and comes back with a huge bowl covered with a cloth. She steps on a stool. This is serious.

"Everyone, listen." Cô Hạnh holds the bowl high. Is this a taste test? Why does Út look that sickened? She's not a picky eater. I've seen her tear through roasted pigskin. *"Go in pairs and wet your hair out back. I hope each has remembered to bring a towel."*

I'm beginning to panic.

"Each should use enough paste to cover every bit of your partner's hair. If we keep suffocating each potential lice egg before it hatches, we should never find crawling black specks."

LICE???? EGGS????

Everyone follows directions, except for the anxious Út and the in-shock me. Út's mom puts her face right on Út's, still gripping us. *"You thought you were so clever two months ago, but not this time. Remember, if you shave your head again your father will take you to his shrimp camp and you'll have the same future as the boys in the village who do not study well. Do you want that?"*

Út can barely hide her smirk. She's already told me Froggy keeps her here, but if someone were to force her to go play in the ocean air and be elbow deep in hatchlings, it wouldn't be the end of the world.

"Now put on the medicine and sit and chat like every girl here. It stings a little, but the result is worth one hundred times the inconvenience."

IT STINGS????

We are steered to the back. There are towels for those who forgot, of course. We bend forward and pour warm water over each other's head. It feels surprisingly good. Cô Tâm hovers behind us.

Back inside, Cô Hạnh takes over. *"I'll manage you two. Bend your head forward, like this, I need to see your nape and behind your ears especially."*

My eyes water just smelling what's in the bowl. Grainy, smashed something is steeped in a clear potent broth, smelling like it would catch on fire if there's an open flame all the way in the next room.

Smeared, eyes rimmed red, Út gets her head wrapped in a plastic bag. My turn. I back away, but what good does that do?

"What do you do for lice in America? Here, I mix rice wine with the pounded seeds of quả na.*"* Cô Hạnh holds up a fruit with thumbprint circles all over its green skin and lots of beany black seeds. Mom would be so proud that nothing has been wasted. I wonder what Cô Hạnh does with the green peel? It has some medicinal purpose, no doubt, and, please, let me never find out.

"We do this every month, and in years we have not had lice in our village. You have to kill the possibility of even one egg. If allowed to hatch, we would have to shave our heads and burn all the hair. Prevention is so simple, but Út shaved her head because she would rather sit in the pond with her pet than here with us. Her mother screamed so loud that the next village heard and would have thrown that frog into the fire pit if I hadn't intervened. She wants her girls to be beautiful.

But she did not know to get braces for Lan until it was too late, just a slight overbite, no big flaw on Lan's beauty, but to her mother . . . She did get braces in time for Út, then to have Út turn herself into someone ready for a Buddhist nunnery, oh."

Why is she talking so smoothly to someone who isn't supposed to understand? A distraction, a trick, so I won't . . . OWWWW! IT STINGS!!! Tears. Lots of tears. No wonder Út shaved her head. I'm thinking about it too.

"Take a deep breath, breathe out, it's over."

The sting does lift. Is she a magician? My head feels tingly and cool. Still, if she's going to market this potion, she has got to tone down the initial shock.

"Go sit," Cô Hạnh directs me toward Út, pouting in a corner. I join her in pouty protest. She lets me.

CHAPTER 18

It's been the longest day ever and it's just nap time. Út disappeared as soon as she washed her hair, and who knows where Anh Minh went. I had to walk back to Bà's all by myself with the lunch basket. Usually, Út and I bring it and eat with Bà.

Neither of us wanted lunch today. Now that I've joined Bà inside the net, my stomach decides to grumble. How can I be hungry after eating my body weight at breakfast? Very spoiled, this new appetite of mine.

Bà gets up from the bed and I follow. In the basket sits my and Út's favorite, *bánh ít*, steamed sticky rice cakes with mung beans and pork wrapped in a banana leaf. The best part is peeling off the leaf, which imprints the rice with the color of light jade and the smell of spring. I have to bring one to Út.

Bà knows. So excited, I lead Bà back to bed, tuck her inside the net even though she doesn't believe in afternoon mosquitoes, grab two *bánh ít*s, and run as I ninja-up.

In Cô Hạnh's back pond, Út is not under our willow tree, where Froggy usually naps in the water just offshore. Of course Froggy is gone too.

I look across the pond. In the heat, in certain half-shade, half-bright spots, vapors rise into nothingness. I have an urge to walk across the water and hold onto the vapors, as if that could ease the loneliness I feel. The rice cakes call out, promising fresh-leaf, springtime mellowness, but I would never eat mine without Út.

Wait, is that a canoe? Someone is leaning over, face almost in the water.

I scream, "Út, Út," and run to the landing plank. I wave her over, offering the cakes as bribes. Is she paddling away? How rude! To think, I was fuzzy with warm thoughts about her. Well, I will go out there. How different can canoeing be from paddleboarding? There just happens to be a wooden canoe nearby, pulled up on mud. I push it into the water, throw the cakes in, jump in myself, never mind that I'm muddying Chị Lan's silky flowy pants. Later, I will scrub them, but right now I've gotta row. I actually go forward. Bonus.

Almost side by side, I throw a *bánh ít* into her canoe. Of course, she picks it up. Who wouldn't? My canoe bangs into hers. Shushing me, she points to the other side of her canoe. I can't see so I stand up and step into hers. She's shaking her head. Calm down, I want to tell her, I've paddleboarded on waves.

In the water, Frog lounges on a lily pad shaded by weedy plants and is more enormous than ever, sinking the broad leaf underwater. So that's who Út's been talking to. No wonder she's so obedient to Cô Hạnh, who owns Froggy's true home. This must be where Út found her froggy sac.

Next to Froggy sits a frog with the same slimy brown-green skin but much thinner. How sweet, Froggy has a friend. Are they wrapping their short front legs around each other? I have to lean over to get a closer look. Út yells something like *"Đừng, đừng,"* which sounds almost like "don't, don't," and before my brain can translate it the canoe is rocking big-time and *PLOP*.

Of course I can swim; I'm a beach girl. But not in ninja gear. I realize I'm swallowing POND WATER, which Dad said is full of bacteria, parasites, invisible worms . . . all foreign to my body.

"HELP!" I hold one arm high while treading water, like I learned in swim class. Another gulp. The water tastes exactly like diluted rotting plants, earthy and sluggy and a bit bitter. A hand rips off my mask, then my hat. I'm pushed above water. I love air! Where's the lifeguard float? I see a blurry fat frog, then realize there'll be no float. So I yell louder. Someone grips me, hard. It's Út, dragging me toward one of the canoes. We hold on and she paddles us to shore.

As soon as I climb onto Cô Hạnh's back porch, I throw up in front of a huge, loud gathering. Isn't everyone supposed to be napping? If there's anything worse-tasting than scummy pond water, it's vomit. Út, looking worried, slaps me on the back. Seeing this, the villagers slap me on the back too until Cô Hạnh makes them go home. She takes one arm, Út the other, and they escort me to the bathroom. I smile at Út to mean I'm glad you were there, and she nods back to mean of course.

Cô Hạnh gives me a clean pajama-ish set and I'm allowed alone time in the bathroom. I feel peaceful with the world, a little pond water is nothing. And yet something is tugging and tightening on my left calf. I pull up my pants. A gray lump pulsates, getting bigger and turning light pink. I take the end of a toothbrush and flick it off. It won't budge. I poke it really hard. One end of the lump rises up and says hello with a stretchy, bloody mouth.

The room spins. I drop to the ground. My cheekbone hits first.

"Miss, wake up, please, the entire village is concerned with your well bein'."

The voice darts into me, dragging along a twang. Yes, Anh Minh is here and he's sorry.

The left side of my face hurts like it interfered with a swinging racket, leaving a tennis ball where my cheek used to be. I'm sure I'm black and blue. Is this enough of an emergency to get sent home? I'm so going to text a picture of the bruise to Mom.

I sit up really fast, remembering something much worse than a bruise. Somehow, I'm on a hard bed on the second floor where lots,

I mean lots, of maybe-relatives have returned.

I poke an index finger around my left calf.

"No worries, miss, be assured your leech has been appropriately dealt with."

I don't want to know.

"Cô Hạnh rubbed on a bit of salt and your leech released instantly."

Stop talking.

"Your leech had not attached for long . . ."

"It's not MY leech!"

Of course, the supertranslator does his job. The crowd roars. Go away, now!

The crowd backs off. Wow, am I so powerful? No, they've parted a path for Cô Hạnh. She sits next to me on the hardest bed ever, holding a steaming bowl smelling of herbs and stewed bark, so basically compost in a cup. Oh, it's going to be bad.

"Drink this and it will ease the cramps."

I wait dutifully for the translation then announce, "I don't have cramps."

The room erupts with advice. I will be sick, they admonish, by tonight for certain, my stomach cannot fight such strong home-grown parasites, they warn, true Vietnamese guts would have no problems, they brag, but mine, oh . . . so much sweets in the intestines. I drink so the voices will hush.

BITTER. Throat-scorching, gag-inducing thick brown sludge that tastes like . . . where's the perfect word when I need it? Cô

Hạnh holds my nose and tilts my head back until I gulp for air and am forced to swallow every little drop. I'm bruised and possibly parasite ridden, why is she torturing me? She smiles and calls it herbal medicine. I call it child abuse.

"Nothing to eat, drink only hot water until your stomach expels the foreign elements," Cô Hạnh says.

I wait for the translation and turn to Anh Minh, "Tell her I have not eaten since breakfast. A little something?"

The whole room erupts in tut-tuts.

"Miss, we are in agreement you must not feed the source of your pain."

"I don't feel pain."

More tut-tuts ring out as Cô Hạnh shoos everyone out of the room. *"Take a nap. You will need your strength."*

I feel fine, but I might as well lie here, daydreaming about the *bánh ít* calling my name from the bottom of the pond.

CHAPTER 19

I wake up, not that afternoon, but the next morning, starving. That sludgy med knocked me out. Bà always said the more bitter the medicine, the better its healing power. Why couldn't Cô Hạnh stir in some sugar? Or honey, that's all natural. Oh, it's this kind of thinking that has turned my blood into nectar for the buzzers. Why is everything that's good for me so painful?

I smell Chinese sausage, popping in its own fat. Yum. I swing my legs off the wooden plank, not dignifying it with the word *bed*. A *đi văng* is its official name, one of those words left by the French, *divan*. BTW, the French are responsible for all those pesky accent marks. Some time ago, Anh Minh started to tell me how and why but I blacked out.

This *đi văng* is made of solid ebony wood and is passed down to the child who nurses the parents through old age. Why would such a bed be a prize? All it does is make you hurt.

Before I can get up, Bà swoops over from somewhere and shakes her head. *"Listen to your stomach, listen to what it needs."*

On cue, my stomach instantly coils. PAIN! A whole den of snakes is doing somersaults in there. It's as if they've awakened in a hostile environment and they're beyond mad. If I could reach down my throat and yank out each twisty one, I'd do it. OOOWWW!

Cô Hạnh appears with yet another bowl of hot compost. *"Drink, you will feel pain lifting before the medicine even cools."*

Before I can react she tilts back my head and holds my nose, so to continue my mortifying life I have to suck in a breath and thus swallow. And swallow some more. When she releases me, I'm thinking of all kinds of colorful words . . . but she's right, I feel better. The contorting knots are turning back to plain old intestines. Even my cheek aches less. Wow, Cô Hạnh should totally package and sell this brew, but it would have to come with a personal tormentor to hold your nose and force it down your throat. As for her lice paste, that would have to be sold with a personal gripper to hold you still while your scalp burns.

Út stands at the edge of the bed, rubbing her head. I had not noticed but her buzz has grown just enough to seem almost pixie chic. No, *chic* is too strong a word. She waves first. I wave back.

Suddenly, my stomach rumbles, building up a sense of urgency. I jump off the bed and run to the bathroom. Cô Hạnh is right behind me. *"Expel all you can, it'll only help."*

You'd think after an emergency trip to the bathroom, I would be allowed peace and tranquillity and a sliver of privacy.

But no.

Maybe-relatives, lots of them, have surrounded my plank, pushing Bà and Cô Hạnh to the back. They part so I can lie down, then hold Anh Minh in place as the official translator. Whispers grow louder, until all across the room they are debating the details of my . . . fine, I'll just say it . . . diarrhea. With much regret, I understand every word. It's excruciating to hear each analysis once, then I have to endure it again in translation.

"Black and loose means the parasites are still in there," so begins my personal translator. "They advise you must release until your offerin' turns light brown, yellow is best. You want a tender consistency, not too firm or too soft. Too yellow could mean . . ."

KILL ME NOW! If I can just be alone, pleeeassse, I promise to admire my parents out loud, I will never complain again, I will stay here and like it, I will speak only Vietnamese, I will be so perfect once home that my parents will beg me to stay overnight with Montana so I can get into trouble and be more human.

"Often yellow does not eliminate until the following day, first a greenish brown . . ."

I grab Anh Minh by the collar. "I will drink whatever and sleep however long, but I never ever want to speak of my bodily functions again, agreed?"

I'm near tears. Anh Minh flusters and says, "I apologize for all of us. Of course you should have privacy."

I have him now. "You're not still mad at me, are you?" I clutch my stomach and moan.

He isn't such a pushover. "I had plenty of time to email my roommate while waitin' in Hà Nội, miss. His sister, your exact age, and her friends do not wear the revealing undergarment that you tricked the girls here into making."

"It got crazy, but I swear, some girls do wear them at my school. I'm not lying." I clutch my stomach again.

"You told the girls all Americans wear them."

"So sorry, really. I got carried away."

"I watch everythin' I do and say because . . ."

"Isn't that tiring?"

He looks puzzled, like no one has ever asked him that before. For once, he has no reply.

"Do you have to worry and be so serious all the time? Can't you just be you?"

He laughs. "That line exists in just about every Hollywood movie. It is impossible to think of just me when the whole village has sacrificed for me to study overseas."

"That's a lot of pressure."

He nods. There's nothing else to say. The ever-present crowd is quiet for once, listening to our every word.

It occurs to me Anh Minh doesn't get to mess up ever or pout or throw a fit. If he's so obligated to pleasing everyone, how does he know what he wants? I'm afraid to ask him though, that's probably another really American-movie question.

"I'm sorry." That came out automatically. "Do you want me to apologize to the girls?"

"That would be proper. They really want to stop wearin' those unfortunate things but they don't want to displease you."

"I hate thongs."

He laughs really hard. "Anyone with a normal anatomy would."

The crowd roars. They are beyond weird.

Út comes pouncing in with one red fruit held up in reverence. Froggy's basket occupies her other hand. Everyone stares at the fruit like at a gigantic ruby.

"Is that quả sung*? Is it ripe? Chú Tư gave you the first of the season?"*

Út beams, no need to speak her answers. Still holding the fruit high, she takes Froggy out of his basket and plants him on my chest. He's really heavy and smells like a soggy mushroom. Has he gotten even fatter?

"Ready?"

I nod because the new me is trying to be agreeable. Út, though, is addressing her slimy beloved. She breaks open *quả sung*, which rips apart from the slightest tug and reveals deep red meat with tiny white seeds. Froggy actually lifts himself up. From this opened gift, a bunch of fruit flies do what they do, they fly out. As in out of the fruit. Froggy flicks each and every little snack into his wide, grinning mouth. I barely feel his bulky mass move; he's that good.

Everyone claps. Me too. That might be the coolest thing I've seen in Vietnam. I admit if I saw on PBS *Nature* a bunch of people clapping as a frog snaps up every bug that escapes from a fruit, I would think they need help. But here, with every maybe-relative elated, I would have to be made of steel to not join in.

Cô Hạnh takes the plum-sized fruit and cuts it into dozens of tiny bites. Everyone gets a taste, oohing and ahhing about how it's sweeter than sugar. Everyone except me. I'm still officially a worm-infested invalid.

Út finally lifts the bug catcher off my chest. Ah, to catch a full breath. In front of me Út takes a bow, signaling that the PBS *Nature* episode was for my benefit.

CHAPTER 20

Vietnam is a land of contrasts. Either nothing happens or everything happens. Guess who just arrived and got everyone stampeding to the front yard? This includes Bà, who can't run but she sure is moving it.

DETECTIVE NABS RELUCTANT GUARD

I might go into headline writing. Drama, suspense, that's me.

Told to stay put on the bone-grating plank, I wait for the room to clear, then sneak down to the first floor. Hiding to the side of the front door, I can see and hear everything. I'm the greatest spy on earth, oh yeah! Legs a little wobbly, but I can stand. My empty stomach is firm, nothing flipping around in there. My cheek has deflated to a golf ball. I'm going to tell Dad about that foul but miraculous med. But even Mom's scouts are having trouble reporting about him. He has moved deeper into the mountain.

Everyone, for once, hushes, standing back and watching the detective lead the guard to Bà. What is it about Vietnam that produces the thinnest men ever? The guard rivals the detective in wrinkles. His cheekbones protrude like two lightbulbs and, under his shirt, knots actually poke up on his shoulders. I can't possibly guess his age to know how to address him. Is he of Ông's generation or Dad's?

The guard bows deeply and Bà nods her head. They look speechless to finally be breathing the same air. Even the effusive detective stands silent.

Cô Hạnh, who must be the most efficient person on earth, comes running with a little rattan table and other people bring three chairs. A pot of tea, three cups, a plate of peeled, white fruit with lots of supershiny, oblong, black seeds. So hungry, my mouth waters even though I know the seeds are mashed into a fiery concoction that will burn lice and scalps off human heads.

The three sit outside my door, with Bà and the guard staring right at but not seeing me. It's so quiet I can hear breath and birds and the breeze against leaves. C'mon, speak!

The detective talks first, of course. This will take a while. Bà sits up straight, hands folded on top of each other on the table. Her features hold steady, willed to stay frozen. But she can't control her eyes. They seem hopeful and tired and firm all at once. *"Please, allow me to listen,"* she says.

The guard clears his throat. I think he's a little afraid of Bà, whose eyes are piercing him. He gains time by taking tiny sips of tea. My heart flip-flops like a just-caught fish. Talk, please.

"To begin, allow me to say I never thought this day would arrive." He takes more sips.

I can understand. Thank you, universe! Every atom in my body lets out a sigh. Forced to fly across the world and spend weeks in this mosquitoey hotbed, at least I get to listen to the conversation of a lifetime.

"Also allow me to say I understand our meeting carries the weight of mountains. To be clear, I never regarded your husband as an enemy. Something about his face made him as familiar to me as an older brother, as I was just out of school in the spring of '68. We spoke the same accent. We ate the same rotten rice. We stayed in the dark tunnels for hours, and at times days, as bombs shattered the earth above our heads. I had come south for the attack at Tết and was told to stay. My assignment was to lengthen a section of the tunnel that led to a pond. We could not survive long without water. Even if we couldn't cook for fear of releasing signs of smoke, we could survive by sipping.

"By calculation, if I could dig thirty centimeters a day southeast from the storage chamber, angling up by thirty-five degrees to allow for flooding, I would reach the pond in six months. I was given a block of wood and a piece of metal as thick and long as my wrist with a pointy end. By chiseling into the earth, chipping away fingernail bits at a time, I found I could not meet the daily requirement even if I worked without pause day into day. This was during the height of the dry season and the clay earth in Củ Chị might as well have been cement,

brilliant for holding up a tunnel but cruel to the joints and muscles that labored to remove it."

OMG, what are the chances of me meeting the second wordiest human on the planet? Yet here he is. At least I can understand most of what he's saying. C'mon, what happened to Ông?

"My commander took notice and brought help. A prisoner, shriveled and cracked, wearing the same brown set we wore, but his feet were bare. I suspect someone of high rank had admired the pants, shirt, and shoes he had once worn."

Bà straightens her back.

"He was given the same metal piece, the same chunk of wood. One of us would rest in the storage chamber, a dugout big enough for several to lie down or stand up, while the other would disappear into the dark passage and scrape at the earth. Just the two of us, taking turns resting or digging by day, and if the universe had mercy on us there would be no sounds of helicopters by night and we could come up to cook and stand and breathe the clean beauty of natural air."

"Did you ever hurt him?" Bà asks, her voice sharp, taming down emotions.

"Never. I was a guard in title only. Every other aspect, we were brothers. Every misery he suffered I suffered. I have no doubt I was assigned to dig an unimportant corridor because I had not shown enough bravery in battle. I was often criticized for thinking too much and dulling my mind from its singular purpose, which was to win at all costs."

"Let's not talk of war. How was his strength?"

"We had skin blanketing bones. We shared one sack of moldy rice and at night we would boil one palmful and remove the black floating bodies of whatever had infested it, then we added the edible greens we could find. Once in a while a villager would donate a sweet potato. Until this day, I cannot think of a more perfect food. We boiled it and drank the brown, sweet broth. Then we divided the potato into two equal parts. By taking tiny bites, not bites but scrapings, we could savor it until the last hint disappeared into our saliva. By will our halves lasted until the sun began to rise and we had to retreat back down. But those mornings, with sweet potato mashed into our taste buds and the memory of a breeze circling us, we felt as if we had been granted the sky. We dug with a bit more power as the sweetness lingered on our tongues and the mellow smoothness rested in our nostrils."

Bà smiles, just the tiniest bit.

"He told me he was accustomed to having a steamed sweet potato every morning, without fail, half to eat at home, half to bring to work as a snack. I sensed it was his wife who saw to this routine, but he never referenced her, as if a real mention of her would soak up what little oxygen we had in that inferno of a tunnel and leave us breathless with sadness. I never imagined such a wife would be sitting in front of me all these decades later."

I know the sweet potato story. Bà told me that Ông had stomach troubles and sweet potatoes soothed and kept him full. I see her eyes blinking, as if remembering too.

"He told me of his seven children. His oldest boy Mong would have turned fifteen that year, a boy kindhearted and shy and who

now carried the family with his every step. Nhớ was next at thirteen, stubborn and wild but his saving trait was his devotion to his mother. His oldest girl Em would have been eleven, so smart she did her big brothers' math work and still had time to jump rope. His next two girls, Đếm and Từng, were nine and seven but might as well be twins. They were the same height, ate the same foods, read the same books, cried at the same moments, and had fits of laughter about occurrences no one else heard or noticed. He gave Hạt, who would have turned five, a tricycle in the weeks before he left. The boy rode it all day and all night, with the family falling asleep to the sound of squeaky little wheels going around and around. His baby boy, Mưa, was just talking and by then would have begun babbling sentences. The first time he told me their stories he had been separated from them one year eleven months and eighteen days. Each time he retold their stories he would recalculate their time apart."

Bà raises a hand as if she can't bear to listen anymore. *"How long was he with you?"*

"One dry season."

"You last saw him when?"

"I never could learn his system of keeping a calendar by plucking the hairs on his toes and calves. It was close to the end of the dry season because we yearned for rain so much we tasted it in our own sweat."

"Saw him last when?"

"My apologies for a habit of hoarding words. After all, they are free. That last night we had been breathing real air for just a few hours. It was our routine to drag ourselves to the pond and cook our

rice. Water and air still seem to me the two most beautiful gifts on our earth. The previous night we had spent completely underground because helicopters circled all night. So we desperately needed to breathe. I still cannot fully describe the air in the tunnels. Of course, it was skin-peeling hot, but that, the mind will acclimate to. To say it stank with human waste and rotting flesh is just voicing the obvious. But I cannot describe what it was like to inhale stale, trapped, smokey, fragile oxygen. We simply did not have enough. Our chests hurt after each inhale and our minds clawed for more air, but there was none. It was a hunger that gnawed at every pore in our beings. That last night aboveground the air was particularly lovely, a breeze, such luxury is a breeze, and the sweet linger of roasted corn from some nearby hut. We talked that just smelling it, never mind getting to eat it, was a gift from some spirit who remembered we were still alive. Then too soon we heard the helicopters again. I limped back to the tunnel and thought he was behind me. Neither of us could walk well from lack of food and air and from too long under the reign of invisible tunnel creatures that feasted on and inside us. He had a cough that wanted to devour his lungs and intestines. The cough persisted as long as I knew him. Only when I reached the tunnel's secret entrance did I realize I had been limping alone. I went back for him but could not get him to stand, much less move. He said 'Enough,' that he was a human being not a mole, and that while he had learned to live without sunlight, he could not relinquish air. I pulled at him. By then, American planes were following their helicopters, and the first bombs could be heard."

Bà gasps. That gives everyone else permission to do so too. Except me. I'm confused. The Americans and Ông fought for the same side, the South, right? But if the Americans found Ông with the guard they would think he's a Communist too, I think. The Communists were from the North but they were also in the South. Where is PBS when I need a review?

"I pulled again and he slapped my hand. Red and blue flares reflected in the pond. The bombs were quite near, opening up like parachutes inside my eardrums. He pulled back his rot-thin pants to reveal feet and calves swollen with pus and darkened with insect bites. 'Enough,' he said again, and coughed so deeply I was surprised he still had lungs. The helicopters were now over our heads. I scrambled to the tunnel. I glanced back at him sitting by the water. The flares rained down to reveal the face of a man in a deep inhale."

"You left him out there?" Bà asks, and stands up. Oh-oh!!

"I pulled but he . . ."

While the guard fumbles for words, Bà leans over and slaps him across the face. SLAPS HIM!!! Bà never raises her voice, even when I deserve it, and now she has slapped the one person who knows about Ông? The guard's mouth falls open. Everyone sucks in breath.

"You did not perform your duty," Bà says in an iron voice that is not hers.

"I had not the strength to force him," the guard pleads. He's not angry, just panicky like the rest of us.

"You should have dragged him back down, forced him if you

must." Bà's iron voice has shifted into a choke. She walks away. I should follow but I'm supposed to be on the plank. What if she slaps me too? First, she wants to make sure the guard did not hurt Ông, then she wants the guard to use force if needed. Nothing makes sense in a war.

"We never found his body, by the pond or anywhere," the guard calls after her. *"He wrote you a message."*

OMG, that's huge! But Bà keeps walking toward Ông's ancestral home and no one dares to stop her. Did she hear the guard? This makes coming to Vietnam almost worthwhile. Why won't Bà listen to the best part?

"Let me have the letter," the detective demands. He stands up, face rigid. In this kind of emergency, even he omits the poetic nonsense. Thank you!

"It's not a letter that I can carry," the guard says. *"She has to come see it."*

"The letter, now! I have no more patience."

"If you bring her south, I will take her to see it."

Just like Bà, the guard stands up and walks out of the village. Why did he hide the message in the South? Is the message a letter?

The detective releases swirls after swirls of words and gestures, but the guard keeps walking and shaking his head. The detective looks ready to chase and tackle him. But in a contest between two equally leathery men, the younger one will always be able to flick off the older. Even the detective knows this and slumps down on his stool.

If the detective is defeated, this know-everything, been-all-over man, then what can the rest of us do? Everyone starts shouting and running and I hurry back to the torturous plank. With this many people on edge, I'm not about to add to the tension.

CHAPTER 21

By late afternoon:

Bà has shut herself in the blue goddess room.

The guard, whose name I've finally learned is Thượng and I'm to address him as Bác, meaning he's younger than Ông but older than Dad, has disappeared. I can twist my tongue and intestines into several pretzels and still not be able to say Bác Thượng, so I shall continue to refer to him as "the guard."

The detective is frantic, dropping things, running here and there, emailing Dad, shouting into his cell. Yep, the oldest man ever has a cell. Finally, he leaves too.

Cô Hạnh tries to get everyone to sip tea and eat soup, two acts meant to bring about peace and harmony, and failing at both, she goes to give herself a facial.

Út and Froggy retreat to the pond.

Anh Minh has been sent on errands.

That means no one is watching me.

I'm about to report these monumental events to Mom when I realize I left my cell in Ông's Brother's house. A good thing, otherwise the cell would be at the bottom of the pond. But if I'm to have energy to text later, I've got to eat. Seriously, I can feel my cheeks sinking in, even the one recently swollen and still bruised.

I fumble my way to the *phở* stand in the open market. It smells like safety: salty beef broth, sturdy white noodles, sprigs of basil, wedges of lime. I realize I must look pathetic, bruised and pale, standing there swallowing spit. But I can't force my feet to step away. It's the end of the market day and the sun has weakened. Thank goodness few people are around. The *phở* stand owner waves me over.

"What does your stomach tell you? Can you eat?" Of course she knows about my troubles. No one has secrets in Vietnam.

I nod so eagerly my head wobbles like a dashboard doll.

"Eat just noodles and broth, all right? Let's listen to what your stomach does with that."

They are just rice noodles and beef broth, but they are the best rice noodles and beef broth ever. My stomach shreds every bit and demands more. But I have no money. My face tells her. The seller pats me on the shoulders and say, *"It's only the bottom of the pot. Go on home."*

"Cảm ơn," thank you. *"Con qua ngày mai,"* I come here tomorrow. I mean to say I will pay her tomorrow, but those are the words I

know and they will have to do. But four words in a row! I'm getting less Tarzan-ish.

Two girls I recognize from the sewing party walk up, smiling. From their ability to not pick and wiggle, I can tell they know about my talk with Anh Minh and have rid themselves of their thongs.

Without saying anything, they escort me all the way to the cement front yard at Ông Brother's house. There, I step on something: the detective's notebook. Can I be this lucky? The powdery cover has very little leather left, but the pages somehow hold together. The girls think nothing of this find and leave. I hear their flip-flops disappear into the dusk and know I have minutes before an army bearing minuscule swords will start hunting. So what if I could sorta maybe pass for a real Vietnamese in my pajama-ish set, I won't fool the buzzers.

Inside, under a dangling bulb, I flip through inky, tiny handwriting dating from 1975 to now. The detective must be turning his stomach inside out looking for his beloved notebook. I'm so mad at myself for not learning to read Vietnamese. When I get back, I'm going to go to school in Little Saigon. Yes, my parents always nagged me. Yes, I always fought them because each class lasts all Saturday. Track meets that day, and HE is on the boy's team, and . . . you know. Track, though, doesn't last all year.

I crawl inside the mosquito net, arrange the pillows just so. Bà's awake, chanting. When I was little, I used to fall asleep every night to that murmur and the comfort of Tiger Balm and BenGay. I hadn't known how much I missed her until this summer.

"If only I could retrieve the force in my palm."

I hold Bà's hand. *"Không sao,"* no worries, I say, using Bà's constant phrase. Maybe it'll soothe her too.

"In listening, my intestines wrung themselves until I thought they would tear. Imagine Ông coughing and starving, without even a pair of sandals. The guard did not say but I heard between his words that Ông was too weak to have survived even if he had dragged himself back under. I understand Ông's yearning for real air in possibly the last hours of his life, but I was thinking of us. I should not have punished the person who told me what my entire being refused to hear."

"Không thấy người." Not see person is what I say to mean they didn't find his body. Bà understands and sits up.

"How do you know?"

I repeat what the guard said, dramatizing with hand gestures and facial expressions. Bà looks so hopeful and sad and determined.

"Maybe a villager pulled Ông inside his hut, maybe they cared for him or took him to a hospital, maybe he was granted a full stomach, maybe they bandaged his feet. Maybe someone cared for him in our absence."

Bà sounds strangely hopeful.

"Ông sống?" Ông alive?

Bà whispers her frequent word, *"Maybe."*

"Làm gì?" What to do?

"I need to apologize to the guard, maybe . . ."

When I was little, Bà would whisper all kinds of maybes to herself when she thought I was asleep. I remember now. I used to sneak in and sleep with her way past kindergarten, up to third grade even. Deep in the night, I'd hear murmurs of maybe Ông escaped, maybe Ông lost his memory but was healthy and happy, maybe Ông was stuck in a place where no one knew the war had ended, maybe Ông was thinking of us right now.

I listened, even when I couldn't hear every word because some remained in her throat. No matter how I listened, though, I never knew how she would ever come to a point where she'd no longer need the maybes.

Bà squeezes my hand. *"Tell the guard to bring me the letter. I will listen this time. I shall ready my mind to accept that what he knows equates to all we shall ever know and that the time has come to go home."*

"Không thư," meaning there might not be a letter but some other message.

But Bà isn't listening.

Why, why, why do I have such a big mouth? Why couldn't I just keep secret what the guard said, then leave it to the detective to solve everything? We could be going home. Whatever Ông wrote in the South, the detective can bring it to Laguna. He'd like Little Saigon, where signs are in Vietnamese, and the food is so good he'd plump up in no time.

So we're back to waiting for the detective to return with the guard. NO! I'm not sitting around and waiting for our stressed-out, wordy detective to do his one little job. What if he doesn't appear for weeks and weeks? I will get Út to help. We will think of something.

CHAPTER 22

Bà did not sleep all night and neither did I. The more hours Bà had to think about Ông in the tunnel, by the pond, aching for a sweet potato, dragging himself on rotten feet, the more she lay immobile and sighed.

I sat up and tried to comfort her with foot rubs and cold tea then realized she only wanted me to massage Tiger Balm into her temples. That got us through the night. Now at breakfast time, Bà still shows no sign of wanting tea or *cháo*. Of course, I'm starving but playing nice. Út must have brought the basket and left, having been told to not bother Bà or fire up the charcoal stove. The entire village is keeping its distance, giving Bà time to regain her composure.

Such is my life: when I need maybe-relatives to help cheer up Bà, they vanish; when I ached to be alone after the most embarrassing bathroom trip ever, they sardined me.

Bà lies so still that once in a while I have to put my ear next to her mouth to listen for her breaths. That does it, I'm calling Mom.

Ugh, she's not picking up. My message: "emergency. now. help." Surely, that will get her attention.

Within fifteen minutes my phone rings. I jump out of the net, out of hearing range.

Mom gets words out first. "I've got a tough cross-examination, what's the matter? Are you okay? Is Bà? I have to go back in five," Mom whispers, which means she's in the hall peeking into the courtroom. I can see her: gray suit, slick hair, perfectly poised, even if she's exhausted at the end of a trying court day.

"Ông left Bà a letter, and the guard said only Dad can go get it, so Dad must come back right now, like right now."

So I have a habit of exaggerating. But in my logical universe the person who's actually here to endure the stress with Bà gets to relay the facts however she wants.

"Now, now, let's not get carried away. I already talked to the detective and I've hired three scouts to find Dad and drag him back to you."

Why do I have a mom who knows everything?

"It's so not fair. I can't handle this much stuff happening. The guard has disappeared again and I swear every one of my fingerprints has burned off after all that Tiger Balming, and Bà is only taking little baby breaths. Who knows if she's getting enough oxygen? I detest waiting and what if Bà cries and you know I'm only twelve and this is so Dad's problem, not mine."

"Mai, honey. Breathe. I will find Dad; he will come back. But the truth is no one knows what to do. You being there for Bà means you are doing the best thing for her."

"But Mom, what if Bà needs something? What if I do something wrong?"

"Listen to me, you are enough. Sit with her, eat with her, tell her stories, take her on walks, most of all, when she's ready to talk, listen to her. I really have to go, call you later. You're my brave girl. Miss you, love you."

So much for Mom's help. I so don't want to do this, but like Bà has said so many times, *"Cờ đến tay, phải phất."* Flag in hand, must wave it. But I've got to eat first, lots. I can't even wave my index finger right now.

I carry the basket, two bowls and two spoons inside the mosquito net. Not making a big deal of it, I serve myself and Bà and start eating. I chomp and slurp like the detective to inspire hunger in Bà. So far, she's immune. How can she stand it? The sharp dill, the savory catfish, the burning scallions, the heavy fish sauce. I could eat the whole pot. I'm so over being sick.

Finally, even Bà can't stand it anymore and stirs, sitting up. She eats half a bowl. That's not enough sustenance for a two-year-old, but baby steps. Bà sighs and actually smiles at me.

"Shall we take a walk to aid digestion?" She reaches out to pat

my head. That's her way of conveying she's sorry for keeping me up all night. Life is swinging back in my favor; she's feeling guilty. I can ask for anything right now. But control, I'm not one to take advantage.

We need to pay the *phở* merchant, and while there, we might as well eat a bowl or two with extra-hot broth to wilt an abundance of bean sprouts and basil.

I have a bongo belly full of *phở*, making it hard to stroll, especially because I've tucked the decrepit notebook into my waistband. I plan on whipping out the detective's tiny words and distracting Bà should she get moody. Planning ahead, that's the new me.

Three bowls of *phở* floated into me as easily as mango smoothies. Three because portions here are doll-sized to serve a size-zero population. How am I supposed to get beyond lanky in a land where ice cream is made of red beans instead of cream?

We're walking toward the pagoda, Bà's idea. Fine by me. In the middle of the village, under the three-hundred-year-old *cây đa*, people are sitting around, catching the midmorning breeze before going home with the day's groceries. Cô Hạnh sees Bà and springs into action, scattering instructions while clearing a space on a bench. No doubt a pot of freshly brewed tea and some kind of seasonal, perfectly ripened fruit shall appear.

"Không sao, không sao," no worries, Bà tells the crowd, which hovers over her every move. I'm realizing *"không sao"* might be the

most spoken phrase in Vietnamese. Everyone reassuring everyone else everything is all right. It's difficult to be cranky while speaking such a polite and soothing language.

Út is here. I'm so happy I run over and almost hug her but stop myself.

"Phải giúp," must help, I whisper. *"Tìm người canh Ông,"* find person guard Ông.

Út looks skeptical.

Then I say the magical words, *"Ở Hanoi."*

Út jumps up, whips out her writing pad. "How do you know the man is in Hà Nội?"

So that's how you spell Hà Nội? Who knew from seeing the name Anglicized.

I hand over the detective's notebook. As much as he wrote, he must have put the answer in there. Út peers into the detective's tiny handwriting like they contain diamonds. She's very happy with me because I actually see her braces. The writing, though, proves too much for her. She marches over to Anh Minh, who's sorta standing close to Chị Lan, who's attached to Con Ngọc. Triangles are exhausting but I can't stop obsessing over them.

While Anh Minh gets to work, brows scrunching, eyes laser sharp, scanning each line with his finger, Út and I examine the romantic dynamic in front of us. My heart is thumpy, happy. Suspense, drama are back in my life.

Út writes in perfect cursive, "If he calls himself Anh and calls my sister Em, our work has done."

"Huh?"

Út rolls her eyes and writes some more. "That is how he tells her of strong feelings in his heart. If she answers, calling him Anh and herself Em, our work has truly done."

"I CALL HIM ANH," I print clear and big, like a laptop would. We're in secret spy mode, so no whispering in broken Vietnamese.

"For you, *'anh'* means he is like your older brother. For her, it means a strong heart for him she has."

"WHAT DO THEY CALL EACH OTHER NOW?"

"Minh and Lan," Út writes, and gives me a face like, duh!

I could write back, "YOU AND YOUR LANGUAGE ARE SOOOOO ANNOYING," but I choose to rise above.

"SHOULD I CALL YOU JUST 'ÚT'?"

"Or *'mày'* to mean *'you'* and *'tao'* to mean *'me.'*"

I stare at her, probably looking dumb, never having seen these words before.

"*'Mày tao'* is for good friends."

I really stare at her, shocked. I read it again. She did write "good friends." She nods. I nod. *Mày tao* may be the two most beautiful words in Vietnamese.

"Đây," here. Anh Minh yells and jabs a spot on the dusty page.

For real, in pencil, finely scripted, sits an address: *28–30 Đường Ngô Thế Huệ.* OMG, we have an address. It's like the sky opening up.

Út wastes no time. In her notebook she writes, "Follow my lead."

What?

Suddenly, Út clutches one cheek and screams, so loud, as in crying-screaming.

"Owww! It's jabbing my cheek. Owww! I'm bleeding."

Everyone turns white, especially Út's mom. Út falls to the ground, rolls in the dirt, blending it into the dirt already on her wrinkly T-shirt, and clutches her cheek tighter. Hisses of pain. Are those tears? Her eyes are squeezed too tight for me to tell.

All villagers offer opinions, of course.

"Death of me, she's green as spring shoots."

Út screams even louder.

"Blood, did she just spit blood?"

Yes, she did!

"Has she been coughing? Does she have a fever?"

Yes, and no.

"Not so near, she could be contagious."

Too late for the entire bunch, hovering for a close-up.

"My cousin had malaria once, shaking, shaking, his complexion was green like hers."

Noooo! Could I be next? Mosquitoes adore me.

"SSHHH, step back!"

Reason has pronounced itself. Cô Hạnh makes everyone take five steps back. I do it right away. She squeezes Út's mouth, tells her to spit—blood, not a lot at all, but definitely blood—then she pokes an index finger inside Út's mouth, swivels it around, and nods twice. Poor Út, she will soon be drinking something potent and sludgy.

They get up. She sits Út down on a stool that miraculously appears. No doubt, Cô Hạnh has a great team working with her. Út drinks water, opens her mouth for inspection yet again, and finally Cô Hạnh talks. *"A wire from the many that surround her teeth has broken loose and is stabbing her inside cheek. It's quite dangerous and uncomfortable if left untreated."*

"Yank it out," someone advises.

"No, cut the wire first then yank it out," someone else offers.

Út's eyes stretch wide, liking neither idea.

"Chờ," wait, I say and take off down the dirt path, into the convoluted alleys between stacked houses, into Ông's Brother's house, flip open my suitcase, and there it is: dental wax, given for just this kind of emergency. Braces do break and the wax covers the end of the wire so it won't poke someone to death before she can see an orthodontist.

I retrace my steps, breathing hard because my stomach is beyond full. I did not anticipate a track meet. Back with Út, I press the wax over the pokey wire. Emergency avoided. People nod, then wander off.

Hey! These are the same maybe-relatives who freely discussed the minute details of my emergency, but when they could be saying, "Yeah, you saved the day!" or "Imagine if you weren't here!" they choose little head bobs? I'm sweaty, my legs hurt, my heart won't stop ka-thumping. But whatever, this is not about me.

You'd think Út and her mother would be ecstatic, yet they're huddled under a pomegranate tree near the pagoda and are whispering with force. I oh-so-casually ease near them. Spying, so my thing. Some might say they're arguing while trying to hide it, but in this country where a child supposedly never ever disagrees with a parent, everyone has to keep up the PR.

End result: Út is going to Hanoi! Wow, I'm going to try this nonarguing but arguing method.

It turns out Cô Tâm and Cô Hạnh have a third sister, a dentist in Hanoi, who had put on Út's braces. Cô Tâm at first refused to let Út go, but Út insisted teeth go back to being crooked very fast with a loose wire. Add to that, Cô Tâm has always felt guilty that she failed her first daughter in the teeth area. She then vowed to do better for her younger daughter, believing this nearly bald child would need all the help she can get.

Eavesdropping rules!

I, of course, want to go. But I don't know how to ask because Bà needs me and I'm supposed to be magnanimous and nurturing and glued to her. Awful, pretending I don't want to go when I do, really really bad. Út is going, and I know she's up to something, so I have to go.

Út pulls me aside, writes quickly but still in perfect cursive, "Hold your cheekbone. It hurts. Must X-ray. Now."

I whisper back, *"Không có đau."* Not in pain.

"Not I either," she writes.

I look at her like: then what's the deal with your braces?

Út stares me down, eyes narrow and mean. "PRETEND," she stabs the word onto the notebook.

Oh.

"Còn đau," still hurts. I stumble in front of Bà holding my cheek. She inspects my bruise. I know it looks like it's healing just fine, not even purple anymore but light green and yellow, and the ball has completely deflated. But pain has no logic.

"Maybe the bone is broken underneath," someone says. Bless this maybe-relative!

"It's on her face, better to be certain than have a lifetime of consequences," someone else says. Bless you too!

I grimace, moan. I'm sure Bà is thinking what I'm thinking: no one wants to explain to my perfect mom why my face has sunken in. Isn't that what happens when your cheekbone breaks? Bà gently taps my cheek with her index finger. I yell, *"Đau quá,"* such pain!

Now I have to go. Not that I want to leave Bà, but I have to get my face fixed. Bà understands and tells me to go pack. I hug her, even if I'm not supposed to.

Back at the house, she gives me the white envelope Dad gave her. It's full of twenty-dollar bills. Oh yeah, I'm loaded. Bà makes me carry the cash in a home-sewn pouch fastened with three huge safety pins, tied around my waist and worn under my capris. I look like I have a stomach disease.

All sorts of maybe-relatives volunteer to chaperone us, but Anh Minh gets the job because he has yet another appointment at the American embassy.

We will take a van, which will drop us directly at the aunt/dentist's house, where she will care for Út, then take me to get an

X-ray. We will stay one night in the same room with her, then the same van will pick us up the next afternoon. We are to go nowhere without the aunt/dentist and to talk to no one but her and Anh Minh.

Still, the trip has such potential. I pack up everything and pretend I'm going home.

CHAPTER 23

How can a fifty-mile ride last this long?

I'm trapped, hours alone with Anh Minh and Út in the van, with nothing to do but learn the pesky little marks around vowels. We can't even have the radio on. I've seen these annoying marks all my life but didn't know they serve a purpose. Every night I used to copy a whole paragraph of Vietnamese, even though I had no clue what I was writing and the tiny accent marks drove me crazy. Dad really wanted me to do it. So of course I did, perfect daughter that I was.

We're going through the countryside, passing pair after pair of girls holding ropes attached to a bucket, swinging it and drawing water to the crops. I wish I could be out there swinging a bucket, anything to escape Anh Minh, who's cramming an entire year's worth of Vietnamese lessons into my clogged head.

I don't dare try to pout my way out of it, sensing I owe Anh Minh for a little exaggeration about thongs. The punishment is way harsh, but everyone knows payback sucks.

There are only nine tiny marks, but you should see the thousands of ways they can be combined. It's the worst when one is combined with weird vowels, like *phượng*, which requires the manipulation of various parts I didn't even know I had. We're still dealing with the basic ones taught in kindergarten.

"Again, miss. Pay attention. *Ba* plus *dấu huyền* makes your tone go down. *Bà*."

I try and sound like a serious sheep.

"*Ba* plus *dấu sắc* makes your tone go up. *Bá* has many meanings, depending on which word is combined with it."

I try and sound like a surprised sheep.

Anh Minh sighs but perseveres. He is the most diligent human being I know, and remember, I know Bà and Dad and Mom and all those efficient maybe-aunts.

"*Ba* plus *dấu hỏi* makes your tone twist like a question mark. *Bả* means poisoned food."

I try and sound like an frightened sheep.

"*Ba* plus *dấu ngã* makes your tone flip. *Bã* means residue, something chewed and left over."

I try and sound like a sheep falling over.

"*Ba* plus *dấu nặng* makes your tone clog in your throat. *Bạ* means at random, whatever."

This one is my favorite. I get to say "whatever" while sounding like a constipated sheep.

"Miss, are you really tryin'?"

I've always thought these little marks are like decorations, a way to call attention to yourself like people who spell "Amy" as "Aimee" or "Aimy" or "Aymee" or "Amee." A bit forced, but whatever, or *bạ*. The key to making that tone is to close your glottis, which Anh Minh says is the opening between the vocal cords at the upper part of the larynx. This is how he helps me.

"If we were to do away with these little accent marks, no one would notice. I mean . . ."

"MISS! Vietnamese would not be Vietnamese without them, and they are called diacritical marks, not accent."

I've never seen Anh Minh get this red. My head bobs in agreement, so fearful he'll turn magenta and rush to explain the difference between dia . . . whatever and accent marks.

"Let us have examples then." He calms down enough to ask, "What is the name of your mother?"

"Renee."

"Her name at birth."

OMG, I know she legally changed her name but I have no idea from what unpronounceable one. That's something I should know. How embarrassing.

"What is the name of your dad?"

"Ray, I mean Mưa."

"You are saying *mưa* with *dấu móc* that means rain. Just

plain m-u-a means to buy."

"That doesn't sound so bad."

Út writes, "He has strong extra feelings because classmates destroyed his name."

I give her my "go on, do tell" face.

Writes: His true name is Nguyễn Minh Dũng = Bright Bravery.

Anh Minh interrupts. "Not important. We still have much more to learn."

I encourage Út again with my "go on, do tell" face.

"In English his name is Dung Minh Nguyen, pronounced Dung Mean Nugent = mean piece of poop."

I'm not about to laugh, seeing Anh Minh's face. I'm not about to say anything either, afraid I might laugh. But I totally understand why he would go by his middle name. I too would choose to be called mean rather than a piece of poop.

"You think it is funny, miss?"

I shake my head. Really, I have not laughed.

"Mai Le, I am certain you know means spring flower sticking out its tongue. You have to put *dấu mũ* on *Lê* to have a proper family name. When I see a word without its marks, I can make up whatever I want."

Út starts writing.

"Mái Lẻ = uneven number of roofs"

Big deal.

"Mải Lễ = devoted to ceremonies"

Boring.

"Mãi Lé = forever cross-eyed"

Anh Minh laughs.

Hey!

I suddenly appreciate my parents so much. Not only did they come up with a first name that could be flipped biculturally, they chose one without any pesky marks. And who wouldn't love to be named after a flower that blossoms at the first sign of spring? As for my last name, I will from now on write Lê with a little hat over the *e*. Think of it as adding Vietnamese-style sunblock.

I hear an invasion of beeps and we come to a traffic jam. Finally!

"Yes, Hanoi!" I yell.

"Actually, miss, it's Hà Nội, two words, the first word the tone goes down, the second word the tone . . ."

"Oh, *bạ, bạ, bạ*!"

Anh Minh and Út look appalled, like they don't understand me, or maybe they do, but whatever, let me enjoy my cloud of toxic fumes from thousands of lawless mopeds in peace.

CHAPTER 24

Hanoi, I mean Hà Nội, is just as noisy, smoggy, dizzying, crowded, stinky yet alive as I remembered. Now that I'm no longer shocked by the maneuvers of every moped, I notice that just about every house is built in the stacked style like Cô Hạnh's. It's confirmed. One architect designed for the whole country. But each distinguishes itself by the height and the paint. There's one that's seven stories tall in light purple with dark purple trims—a first grader's dream birthday cake.

Our driver slips into traffic, beeping and inching along with the best of them. By the time we are dumped in front of Út's aunt's house, five stories tall in traditional red and yellow, I wish I had accepted one of Bà's seven Tiger Balms. Instead of worrying about smelling like menthol, which of course smells just fine on Bà, I should have worried about the embarrassment of searching for a barf bag.

We walk into the house and it smells painful and mediciny, just like a dental office. That's because the entire first floor is a dental office. Behind a white mask, for the purpose of hygiene not sunblock, a woman tells us to go rest on the second floor. Út calls her Cô Nga, so she must be the aunt/dentist.

The second floor is one big bedroom with lots of foam mats on the floor and dressers along the walls. Weird decoration, but really really clean. Someone brings us fruit and tea, of course, and we are told to take a nap. But we haven't had lunch. Anh Minh puts down his bag and backs out.

"My apologies, I must take my leave and get to my appointment."

"Okay," Út says, and obediently lies down for a nap.

OMG, she understood every word he said.

"Game over, smarty! You understand us!"

"No."

"Cut it out, you do too."

She gets out her handy little pad. "I understand Anh Minh when he speaks English in Vietnamese-accent way. I don't understand you because your words are too fast and too twisty."

Me? "What . . . if . . . I . . . talk . . . slower . . . like . . . this?"

"Maybe."

I've been talking like Tarzan in Vietnamese when I could have been speaking English in slow motion? I glare at her. "Why . . .

did . . . you . . . not . . . tell . . . me?"

She laughs a good long laugh and writes, "Your Vietnamese is so funny!!!"

I'm so thrilled I can amuse her. And three exclamation points are my thing, not hers. I almost tell her I can understand Vietnamese, but just wait. We'll see who's funny.

Cô Nga has outstripped Cô Hạnh as the most efficient person on earth. In exactly seven minutes, she tightens both of our braces, scrapes around in there, asks us if we're in pain, and while we're still nodding she has shooed us off her chairs. A snaky line of patients is waiting.

"What else have I promised your mother?" she asks Út, who points at my cheek. Cô Nga grips my chin, inspects the almost-gone bruise, and calls for someone.

"This is Quỳnh Huyền. She will see to your needs. I'm much too busy, not enough time to eat even." She waves her hand and we're back on the second floor with the assistant attached to an unpronounceable name.

Chị QH doesn't have time either, expecting us to listen, keep up, don't annoy her, and never tattle. In the time it takes a normal person to present these rules, she'd said them in perfect Vietnamese and accented but impressive English. I'm dizzy.

"Agreed?"

Út and I barely have nodded and off we go. We don't have time to tell her Út can understand Vietnamese-accented English. Besides, it's fascinating to see someone's mouth move that fast.

In the courtyard, Chị QH rolls out a pink moped. Bright pink. Her clothes are girly too: black skinny jeans, a tight sequined blouse, and sandals with heels. But nothing about her manners is girly.

"First, I have to dress you two in different clothes or street kids will target you as dumb pots of gold," she says in two languages. Út and I are about to get offended when she whistles the loudest whistle without using a whistle. I have to learn that.

Five mopeds appear with three boy and two girl drivers.

Chị QH points to a girl in jeans and sandals just like hers, but the sequined blouse is purple not white. *"I need you for three hours, perhaps more, fifty?"*

"Chị, how about one hundred, I can make that much on one trip to the airport."

"Sixty-five or I'll get her." She points to the other girl, who is nodding furiously. The first girl revs up her engine.

Are they doing some kind of weird math? I don't dare ask because Chị QH has pointed to me and the seat behind her. She head hooks Út toward the other moped. They give us helmets although they aren't wearing any. Maybe it's an age thing. I have no idea how old the girls are, late teens to late twenties? We all pull out sun masks. Chị QH rips ours off.

"Use these," handing over new ones. Apparently, masks are

supposed to cover only your nose and mouth and be in colors close to your complexion. It must be a city/country thing. Off we go and I'm even more dizzy. Things move fast in the city.

We stop at a building that has a roof but is open on all sides. The other driver has to stay outside to watch the mopeds. Inside, there are three stories, with greasy escalators to move the monumental crowd. In front of each shop sit baskets of goods spilling into the walking paths. Once we manage to get inside a shop, we have to maneuver around other baskets set in aisles. The merchant has to pile baskets on top of each other to make room for me, Út, and Chị QH to stand together.

"Get them pants to fluff out their bones and billowy blouses and student sandals, no heels."

Út and I change behind a sheet the merchant holds up. No comment. But Chị QH has plenty to say about my money pouch. Út is wearing one that's smaller.

"I thought you two had stomach ailments!" she scolds in two languages. Before we can answer, she has ordered two sturdy pouches that can hang unnoticed from our necks under the blouses. Pulling out the pouches in public does not require undressing. Always a plus.

It's miraculous, only in Vietnam do they design pants with puffy pockets that somehow give a skinny girl a full butt. I choose tan while Út chooses brown. Our flouncy blouses are long sleeved but cool and soft. Mine is peach, Út's green. She's the colors of you know who, whom I'm sure she misses very much.

I try to give Chị QH two twenty-dollar bills, but she slaps my hand. "Put that away before you get followed. We'll talk money later with your aunt, and twenties? Really? All this adds up to less than ten dollars, *ma petite soeur.*"

Why is she stacking on French? My brain is at full capacity.

Chị QH wants us to throw out our old clothes, but Út refuses, saying they're her favorite pants. Sighs all around, then everything gets smooshed into a ball and stuffed into a neat space underneath the moped seat.

Next, we stop at an open market with a huge roof to protect against the rain and sun. Although it's open air, the smells are overwhelmingly bad and good, like life itself. Sweat and fruit and boiling oil and raw meat and rows and rows of flowers. The other driver stays with the mopeds. Inside, tons of people mill around everything possible for sale, including stands and stands of food. FOOD! We have not had lunch even though it's late afternoon.

"Excuse me, I don't mean to be annoying, but would it be okay if we bought food? I have money. Actually, I insist on exchanging money so I can pay. Please."

Nothing means freedom like Vietnamese money. You get so much of it. Chị QH looks like at me like I am annoying, but Út is nodding vigorously to help me out.

"If you must tend to your stomachs, then follow me."

We go to a jewelry store. Út and I are too intimidated to protest that I don't even like jewelry and it goes without saying Frog Girl has no use for it either.

"What is the rate today?" Chị QH asks the jeweler.

"Fourteen to one, miss."

"Don't fool me, I know it's nineteen to one."

"That's at the federal bank, miss. Here, we are just a small shop. Fifteen to one then."

Small shop? There are nuggets of diamonds all over the place.

"Enough, eighteen to one."

"Think of the gas I paid transferring the cash and the guards I have to hire." The merchant points at five men holding sticks. *"For you, miss, sixteen to one."*

"Meet you at seventeen or we go to the shop next door."

They settle their weird math. The jeweler opens a fridge-sized steel safe, revealing stacks and stacks of cash. I've never seen that much money. Chị QH asks me for two twenty-dollar bills and hands back a wad that could not all be stuffed into my pouch. I give some to Út.

Chị QH whispers, "You have plenty to play with, don't ever ever pull out your twenties. Understood? I asked for small bills so you can manage. Now put one hundred in your pants pockets. The rest keep in the pouch."

When she says one hundred she means one hundred thousand *đồng*. No one says the last three zeros. One hundred thousand *đồng* equals about six dollars. I love this country! BTW, it's never *dong*, but *đồng*. Tone downward. Dad, for some reason, made sure I knew the difference between *dong* and *đồng* even before we got off the plane. He said it again and again.

Where *is* he? Surely, Mom's scouts have found him by now. I will text as soon as life slows down. With so much happening, I sometimes forget my focus is on getting home, and more immediately on finding the guard. But believe me, guard, home, exhale.

I whisper to Út, "When . . . find . . . guard?"

She writes, "Must wait. Do what they want first, then you get your turn, then I get my turn."

I nod to be agreeable, but I have no idea what she's talking about.

Chị QH leads us to a *bánh cuốn* stand. I love *bánh cuốn*. That's how I learned to eat really spicy, diluted fish sauce. Chị QH orders, tells us to sit exactly here until she gets back, which may be a while, but the merchant has agreed to watch us. I can hear Út swallow a little, me too. She's never been in a big city, and I haven't been left without an adult in so long I instantly panic.

"Don't worry, half the people here know me and Cô Nga, and they all know to not tell her you were left here. Nothing will happen," Chị QH says in two languages. She waves ta-ta, and off she goes.

I'm too hungry to be scared, sitting at a bench with other customers, smelling sautéed dried shrimp and rice flour being steamed to make a crêpe. Heavenly! The others barely notice me. If I don't talk and am sitting down to hide my slankiness, I might pass for a local girl. But Út doesn't sit, instead walks toward the woman who's obviously the owner, standing around chitchatting and doing nothing. Út shakes her head; the woman shakes her head. Oh-oh.

Út comes back to me and says, "Up." She does speak English.

"I'm . . . starving. You too."

"Not good." Funny how Út can speak English when she wants to.

"It smells . . . great. Don't . . . bargain, let's eat."

"Too much."

Út actually walks away, as in away from the stand. I want to smack her. That means running after her. The whole place is jammed with moving bodies.

"What is . . . wrong . . . with . . . you?"

She's madly writing while getting bumped into. "Not pay fifteen for one plate. In village, five, six at most."

OMG, she's bargaining over the equivalent of forty cents. I'm going to kill her . . . later.

We walk to a *bún riêu* stand. I love *bún riêu*, crab blended with eggs and served with a spicy broth and rice noodles.

"Too much," Út writes. "In village, six, seven at most."

"We are . . . in city. Spend money!"

We stop at a *phở* stand. Too much, according to stingy village girl. A *bánh dày* stand. Too much. A grilled-fish stand. Way too much. I come up behind Út ready to choke her. Rethinking, I put my hands in my pockets to control myself. My fingers touch paper. Yes! Pulling out a bill of ten thousand *đồng*, I hold it up to the light. It looks just like real money. The grilled fish vendor sees my money and slyly holds up two fingers, to note that if I pay a bit more we can eat. Út is too busy talking to notice. I pull out a twenty-thousand-*đồng* bill. The vendor nods. Út and I sit.

We eat without talking. I had no idea grilled fish wrapped in lettuce and dipped in fish sauce could be so good. Oh no, I'm not supposed to eat anything raw. Every muscle in my stomach squeezes together. I look around for a bathroom, but everywhere there are people, squatting, stooping, standing, sitting on tiny chairs. My stomach is starting to . . . wait for it . . . nothing. Dad said it would take a little while for my body to acclimate to the bacteria here, so I guess it has. Check me out, I officially have a stomach of iron.

Út is finally full enough to write, "I know how to bargain! 2 plates for 10,000!"

"You . . . are . . . good," I chirp.

We also sample *bánh dày* and *phở* before sitting back down at the *bánh cuốn* stand. Each time I slyly hand over the equivalent of seventy-five cents behind Út's back. Everyone treats us so well and Út feels smart.

When Chị QH does come back for us it's too late to go get my cheek X-rayed.

"How did I become a watcher of two lumps of dough?" Chị QH laments in two languages. *"We'll tell Cô Nga you got X-rayed but have to go back tomorrow to see the results. Nothing about me leaving you, nothing about riding a Honda Ôm. Got it?"*

"What's a *Honda Ôm*?" It means literally "Honda Hug."

Út laughs like she knows so much more than I do.

"You are from over there, aren't you? It's when you hire a Honda with a driver. I was supposed to take you around in a taxi, but it's so slow and jerky and I always get sick. I can't stand them."

I get it, you hug the driver.

CHAPTER 25

Út and I were so tired last night we went right to sleep, skipping dinner because we couldn't eat another bite and no one was eating anyway. Cô Nga just kept working.

In the morning, Cô Nga had already canceled the van ride reserved for this afternoon and called her sisters to give an update. Now she's admonishing Út to never tell her mother that we were left with someone else before handing us back to Chị QH. It's 7:30 a.m. when Cô Nga greets her first patient. Cô Nga's husband runs a cancer ward, where he stays overnight a lot, and their only child is studying English in Singapore. Cô Nga works in her private office every morning and evening. In the afternoon, she puts in time at a government dental clinic for a laughable salary. Doing government work allows Cô Nga to be left alone so she can make private money.

By 7:45, we're in the courtyard, hair and teeth brushed, pouches around our necks, same outfits on. We did wash them last night, and they dried in a matter of minutes on the roof. Út really wants our old clothes back, but Chị QH just sighs.

"I didn't know I'd be sacked with you two again today or I would have bought double of everything," Chị QH laments in two languages.

"Listen," she lowers her voice. "I have to zip through three districts today to gather supplies. I cannot play tour guide. Remember, no tattling."

She whistles and our *Honda Ôm* buddy appears with the same four contenders from yesterday. They bargain, then yesterday's driver inches forward, bringing along a boy on a bright red moped. Chị QH waves ta-ta and off she goes.

"We are your guides for the day," the girl says in two languages. Why does everyone know English better than I know Vietnamese? *"I'm to take you to eat breakfast, then to get an X-ray, then we can do anything for the rest of the day. Would you like to see Chùa Một Cột or maybe something else?"* Út and I can barely keep from jumping up and down. It'll finally be our turn.

"We want to go to Hồ Hoàn Kiếm," Út tells her. I'm shaking my head, but she ignores me.

The girl ignores me too and answers, *"Not today, they're blocking off the area for something."*

Út insists. *"Drop us near there and we'll walk in."*

"Absolutely not, you two would get targeted in two minutes. My

instructions are to guide you at all times."

I can't compete with this level of native-tongue bonding, so I shove a piece of paper at our guide. Prepared, that's me.

"28–30 Đường Ngô Thế Huệ," she reads.

I nod until I'm dizzy and pull on Út's arm, giving her the evil eye that she agreed we would appease my urgency first, then hers. She reluctantly remembers.

Our guides are basically two Anh Minhs with Hondas. The real Anh Minh went back to the embassy before we even got up. No one asked why, understanding that anything having to do with the government sucks up time.

I ride with Chị BêBê. That's her actual name and not the name of a pet. Út gets her brother, Văn, but feel free to call him by his internet name, Van. He says that for my benefit, but please, I can pronounce the miniature bowl over the vowel. He keeps correcting me, though, "Please, call me Van." Fine!

We hug our drivers and off we go. So weird but when you're on a moped and slithering between cars, buses, bicycles, and hundreds of other mopeds, it feels strangely safe even while you're pounded with brake screeches, engine revs, and ubiquitous beep-beeps. No one can go fast in this traffic. We have yet to hit anyone or be hit. Win-win.

For breakfast, we stop at another *bánh cuốn* stand. I love this country! Chị BêBê comes in with us while her brother watches the mopeds. Út bargains while I slip the merchant a ten. At the X-ray place, we are in and out after Chị BêBê tells me to hand over fifty to the receptionist. This must be what movie stars feel like!

By 9:15, we are finally ready to go look for the guard, except Chị BêBê has lost the piece of paper where I wrote the address. It's not like we can Google it.

I'm about to cry. We've come all this way for a brace tightening and some iffy X-rays? But Út offers the address, ever casually, *"28–30 Đường Ngô Thế Huệ."* She does remember the most random things, once reciting the ten most common frogs in North Vietnam, complete with their scientific names, habitats, and characteristics. I'm so relieved I hug her, startling her so much she swats me.

Both of our guides ask, "*Phố nào?* Which neighborhood?"

How would we know? Then Chị BêBê pulls out a smartphone with a GPS! And Dad was worried about me showing off my old rinky-dink cell that's as fat as a wallet and screams FREE? At least the one Mom packed has a keyboard for texting. Why isn't Dad here so I can guilt-trip him into getting me a smartphone? Is he worrying about me? I would ask to borrow Chị BêBê's phone to call Mom but I don't know Mom's number. I know, should have memorized it. Never mind, it wouldn't be right to run up an international charge on someone else's account.

Our guides tell us to hug them tightly and off we go. I love mopeds. On one, I never sweat or get mosquito bitten or can smell much because everything blows behind me, and best of all I pass for a real Vietnamese.

No surprise the address leads us to a rectangle-stacked house, this one in brown with green trims, three stories. I don't have to look at Út to know it reminds her of a certain slimy beloved. A man between the ages of Ông and Dad answers the door. He's actually plump, but that's only compared to the men I've seen here. In Laguna, he'd be normal.

The other three step back and leave me there. I must look panicked because he speaks softly.

"What do you need?"

I have not thought this through. I point to my chest. "Mai."

"Are you from over there? What do you need here?"

I yank Út to stand beside me. "Tell . . . him."

She asks me, *"Name?"*

Anh Minh told me the guard's unpronounceable name once and I promptly forgot it. "Ask . . . for . . . man . . . in . . . tunnel." I make the motion of someone crawling in a tunnel.

The door slams.

Now what? I tell Út she has to knock again and explain about my grandparents and how the detective found the guard and emphasize how I'll get to go home once we find the letter. She refuses. And the two guides say they are just guides, and besides, they must watch their mopeds.

"I can watch your mopeds," I point out.

Chị BêBê shakes her head, amused. "One push and the street kids will have you on the ground and be off with our Hondas."

Desperate, I pull out a stack of *đồng*.

She shakes her head again. "Do you know what Chị Quỳnh Huyền would do to me?"

It takes me a second to understand she's talking about Chị QH. Still desperate, I point the stack toward Út. She pushes it away and nose-puffs. Fine, a bribe is beneath her, but I'm not giving up. "You . . . must . . . help . . . Bà . . . know . . . the . . . truth. She . . . will . . . be . . . sad . . . until . . . she . . . knows."

Út is thinking. She has a grandmother; she knows what it's like to want to please her. Her notebook comes out. "I will try, but no matter what happens, promise me we will spend time at Hồ Hoàn Kiếm."

Of course, but I'm so suspicious.

The sorta plump man answers with a face like he's been expecting us. Út is two sentences into a really moving speech and the door slams. How rude! Út huffs her way back to the guides.

I knock again. He looks like he's about to yell. I suck in a deep breath and jam my foot between the door and its frame.

"Nói con xin. Con là cháu của Ông bị trong hầm." I do the crawling in a tunnel move again. Each little sentence scrapes my brain raw but I have to do this. Breathe, breathe. *"Bà của con tìm Ông đến. Bà của con lắm già. Trước chết Bà của con hết phải chờ."* Where are all these words coming from? I've always known them but never put them together before. I'm so nervous I could pee. *"Xin lầm vui Bà của con. Biết ai có đi Nam đào hầm không?"*

Then I start crying. Stop it, tears! It's so embarrassing, but the possibility of Bà not knowing any more about Ông rips a hole in my gut. Right now, I want Bà to get her wish even more than I want to go home. It's not like I've turned supergood all of a sudden. That's just how I feel. And it makes me convulse with tears. I never knew my nose could produce so much snot or that saliva could pool in my open, twisted mouth. My vision has blurred, but I think the man is changing his expression. He says, *"Chờ đây,"* wait here.

I'm now officially bilingual and can rule the world! The man sends out a boy to bring us four coconuts with straws. The best juice on earth! Then the boy signals all four of us to follow him on his bicycle. We go into alleys where houses get smaller and shorter, and the more we turn, the more the houses start to be made of tin panels nailed to posts. The dirt path turns slippery like there's a greasy film over everything. It smells like sewage. People come out to look at us. Our guides and Út look frightened, so I think I should too.

"This could be a trap to take our Hondas," Chị BêBê whispers to her brother. She calls to the boy on the bike, *"Hey, my tires are getting stuck. Let's go back."*

Út chimes in, *"I left something back there."*

The boy acts like he doesn't hear them and keeps riding on the slippery path. He's an extremely well-balanced individual. All four of us are starting to turn around, which is harder than you'd think, when the boy screams, *"Đến rồi,"* we're here. More heads pop out. I recognize two faces with the deepest creases and the boniest cheeks.

I'm now officially a detective!

The detective yells at each of us, using python sentences that strangle themselves as soon as they enter the air. Yet each of us can't help but grin. The guides because they did not get Honda-jacked, Út because she's in one piece, and me because I rock in general.

I want to hug the detective as he stomps back and forth waving a leathery, angry finger. Needless to say, he got us outta that alley and inside a café ASAP. Best of all, he dragged the guard with us. The detective just happened to be visiting him to convince him, yet again, to visit Bà in her village.

In between all the yelling, I learn the detective's plans:

Ông did write something, but the guard won't tell us what, only that we all must go south.

Somehow, Bà has to be brought to Hà Nội (notice the Vietnamese version).

Somehow, Dad needs to be found and brought to Hà Nội (did you notice?).

Then we will fly south, where all kinds of arrangements have to be made before we can maybe see Ông's writing. Our only hint is the writing does not exist on a piece of paper.

And then, dare I say it, we can GO HOME.

It's all I can do to keep from dancing. Sand, beach, life, see you soon, la la la.

The detective sits down, finally exhausted. The waiter brings him a *cà phê sữa đá*, a potent coffee Dad calls tar water because it's guaranteed to keep an elephant alert. As for me, I'm on my third glass of sugar cane juice, pressed at the counter. It's ssoooo good, especially when they squeeze in a dash of kumquat. I know I'm basically announcing to the insect population to come get me, but who cares, they bite me anyway.

Revived, the detective talks some more but remains seated. *"You two"*—pointing at the guides—*"transport the girls to their aunt's and relay to her my admonition that they must be secured there. I have enough to manage without the additional anguish of them announcing their vulnerabilities to every dire street child in the city. Remember . . ."*

I've stopped trying to understand. But I do love him. With him here, I don't have to plan a thing. Besides, he's not talking to me, so why listen?

I go sit at a back table with the guard, who has not said a word. *"Chào."* I've figured out it's best to say hello without a title or a name. My message still gets across.

"When I saw your group, my heart stopped. How did you find me?"

He doesn't know I'm hiding my ability to understand, so I'm free to converse. Life is actually much simpler this way. *"Plump man angry told. Found house in book he."* I point to the detective.

The guard asks me to repeat my Vietnamese. He must not hear well, leaning forward, listening so hard his facial wrinkles contort like mud patterns at the bottom of a dry creek. Finally, he lets out an "Ah."

"Correct, Ông Ba tracked me to the house of my cousin, who served the war and the war served him well."

I understood every word but don't know what he means. *"Too you war go."*

"I did not possess the skills and temperament to turn such an experience into a benefit. In my youth, every man and woman wanted to help rid the country of intruders. I could not have guessed the cost of actually fighting."

Some words I do not recognize, but I can always spot sadness after years of listening to Bà.

"Choose again war?"

"Good question, my child. I would like to say no, that the human sacrifices were too immense. But Việt Nam is ruling itself, what we all yearned for. And yet who gets to decide what price is bearable?"

I understand every word, but again what is he talking about?

The detective calls us. The guard pats my hand and smiles in a hesitant, regretful way that conveys the world doesn't make more sense just because you get older.

CHAPTER 26

The detective scared our guides so much they are determined to dump us at Cô Nga's and be rid of us forever. But Út, talking louder and faster than I've ever heard, argues that she's so so hungry. Still the guides insist we go home. Út counters that if she doesn't get to eat right now, she would faint in front of Cô Nga, who no doubt would tell Út's mother. The guides have only heard about Cô Tâm and that's enough.

Off we go to the open market, with Van again guarding the mopeds. I want him to eat with us but there are rules here I'm not understanding, so it's best to stay quiet. I get my bills of tens and twenties ready in my pockets. Silent bargaining has become my favorite game.

Right after we eat, Chị BêBê won't listen to anything else from

Út, who babbles that she faked the punctured-cheek incident just so she could visit this lake and look for this one thing that she can't talk about. No wonder Chị BêBê flicks her hand and says she's done with us.

In front of Cô Nga's house, Chị BêBê waves a finger in front of our faces just as the detective had done to her. *"Listen,"* she whispers in two languages. *"If you tell Chị Quỳnh Huyền that we were in an alley in that neighborhood, I will find you! I must remain dedicated and perfect in her eyes. She's helping me get into a school in the city."*

She looks so worried her threat is almost funny. Now the backstories come out. Chị BêBê is working up to asking Chị QH to write a recommendation letter that she's sure will get her into the same dental hygienist program that Chị QH graduated from last year.

"So why are you working as a *Honda Ôm*?" All three shoot me a "hush" look.

"Do you think I run errands and babysit for anyone else?" Chị BêBê is so disgusted with me she's kind of spitting. "It was my only way to get to know her. Besides, my parents and I have to pay for this ourselves. I was two points from a scholarship."

Everything and everybody get so entangled here.

Chị BêBê keeps going. "And do you think Chị Quỳnh Huyền likes running all over the city for supplies? She wants to practice her profession. But Cô Nga already has two hygienists, who are both waiting to hear from dental schools overseas. Cô Nga herself is waiting for a replacement at the clinic, so she can devote herself to her home office."

On and on she talks about who's waiting for what by doing what favors for whom. I try to listen then realize Út isn't listening. She's whispering to Văn, or the international Van, and is obviously pleased with herself. I'm worried.

The siblings wave ta-ta and off they go.

Cô Nga pauses long enough to tell us she has canceled the van again and we are to wait here for further word, grumbling that she had originally agreed to one afternoon, one night, and the next morning, but family . . . how they make her head buzz like a beehive.

She hands us over to Chị QH, still dusty from her supply runs. Chị QH puts us to bed. It's 4:30 in the afternoon.

"But I'm not tired and it's past nap time," I logically point out.

"Then lie still and rest."

I expect some biting indignation from Út, but she bargains that if we could have our old clothes back, we'll go right to sleep. Chị QH claps her hands and says, *"You better be snoring when I return with them."*

"Please put them at my feet."

"Be asleep."

Chị QH leaves. I poke Út. "What's . . . wrong . . . with you?"

"Shhh." She sighs and reaches for her notebook. "Sleep now. This night we cannot."

She moves to a mat all the way across the room. There are seven to choose from. I roll around and against reason fall asleep.

Út shakes me awake. I'm starving. What time is it? It's totally dark. All around us are breathing bodies, where did they come from? I can make out the shape of Chị QH, efficient even in her sleep, taking up just a sliver on the mat. Út puts a finger across my lips and I follow her shadow out of the room. She had grabbed the bag of our old clothes and we change downstairs in the room that smells of pain.

We tiptoe out the front door by sliding a flimsy lock sideways. That's it? Even in Laguna, we have bolts. Is it safe or not safe here? In the dark, I hear buzzers, maddened I'm sure by the smell of sugar in my every pore. Three cane juices may have been excessive, but how was I to know I'd be gallivanting around during the height of bloodsucking hours? I start jiggling like I have a medical condition, which raises the buzzing level. I swat the grayness. Út sighs. Her shadow walks to a plot of dirt that should be a flower garden and picks something. Then she she smashes long leaves between her palms and rubs my arms and legs and face and neck. It smells grassy and flowery and peppery.

I sneeze.

"Shhh."

Like I planned it! I yank the leaves from her and rub rub rub. No bites. I even stick out my arm to tease the buzzers. No bites. I can hear them going insane surrounding me.

"What . . . is . . . this?"

"Ssshhh."

Van appears, all casual, like he often strolls around at this hour with a flashlight. Út follows him. Me too. I've got to get more of these magical leaves. We follow him down the street, around the corner, down another street. It's dark and steamy, but not hot hot, and so quiet I hear crickets and frogs and whatever else that thrive in the dark. We stop at two Hondas guarded by a new girl, called Lulu. What is it about girls and pet-ish names? But I know better than to insult my huggy ride. Lulu looks younger than I do, so I'm definitely not calling her Chị. She's holding a box and net with a long handle. I'm half panicking but can't make eye contact with Út in the dark.

Hà Nội is a different city late at night. We can see the dotted lines on the road, clearly marking two sides of opposing traffic. Other drivers are out too, but not to the point of congestion, so we all follow the rules. Our first stop is at a stand selling *bánh ít*, which is so cheap even Út doesn't bargain.

We're off. As soon as we come near a gigantic pond I'm mega-panicky. I try to get Út's attention on the other moped, but she's pretending to enjoy the night while holding on to the net. The box is sitting on the gas tank, protected by the driver's extended arms.

Út is looking way too happy. We stop in a dark area behind the pond, which is otherwise really well lit. No doubt, Út is up to something illegal, ignoring me on purpose.

"Be back in one hour or we must leave you," Van says in two languages. *"Dangerous to be out."*

Út shakes her head. *"I need you to scoop with the net."*

"Can't. I must guard our Hondas with my cousin."

"Like children!" Út scolds them, then looks at me. *"Đi."*

"Where?"

She marches forth, carrying the net and a box with lidded glass jars carefully separated by towels and plastic bags. Someone has poked holes in the lids. This much premeditation is never a good sign.

"Not . . . going," I yell.

Út marches back and jabs me all over the place with one pointy finger. *"Lá!"* leaf, she yells. I know she means the mosquito-proof leaves, which I must have so I'm forced to play nice.

We walk toward tall reeds that look like a dream breeding site for mosquitoes. But even more disturbing are these glowing dots in the water and the unmistakable ribbits.

"Go in," Út says.

"Lá," I counter.

We realize we each just spoke each other's first language.

"Nói tiếng Anh." I tell her to speak English.

"No."

If she wanted to, she could. But it's pointless to make her. So I'm back to asking where the leaves are. *"Lá đâu?"*

She reaches out and picks some, having put down the box.

Everywhere are shadows of leaves, smelling of pepper.

"What . . . are . . . they?"

She pats her pocket for the notebook. Not there. It must have dropped off somewhere during our ride. She shrugs and pulls me near the water.

"No, absolutely no!"

"Shhh. You are baby!"

Taking the net and one unlidded jar, she wades in, as in into the pond, as in up to her ankles. So this is why she wanted her old clothes. No doubt pond creatures will flock right to her, recognizing their own scent. She makes sure I see her scoop the net into the water then pantomimes reaching into the net and putting whatever she scooped up into a jar.

OMG, I really am in PBS *Nature*.

"NO!"

"Now!" she hisses back.

"I'm not going in there. Remember my last adventure in a pond? No, no. Leeches are not meant to suck on human blood. I shouldn't have to explain this. I'll stand here and keep a lookout but I'm not going in there."

I'm talking just to talk because she's too busy huffing and complaining as she wades deeper into the water. *"What a spoiled, city have-it-all, useless monkey! Why did I think she would appreciate this? I'm still capturing ten of them."* I can barely hear her talking to herself, spitting out saliva in her fury. Fine! I grab two plastic bags, put them over my sandals, hold the bags up, and wade in up to my ankles to listen.

"These are the frogs she should want, if she's so scared of mosquitoes. They lived in the village pond before the fungus that one year. If she would listen, she would know that they eat thousands of mosquitoes plus the larvae every night and they reproduce slowly, five to ten eggs per female per rainy season, so they won't compete with Froggy's kind. They are great hiders, so even if Froggy and his friends fight them, they would hide until everyone gets used to one another."

I pull the plastic bags as high as they'll go, halfway up my shins, and wade in deeper. Please, leeches, go to her, she has homemade yummy salty blood.

"Good friends should do this for each other. I would never have left for Hà Nội if know-it-all couldn't go too. Useless to help her with the cheekbone scheme because she's too precious to get wet. I can't hold everything by myself. All those days when she was with Bà, I left Froggy alone to bring hot food twice a day. Now to think I've chosen the wrong good friend."

I'm right next to her. She looks so upset I think she might cry or hit me with her net. I snatch it just in case. That leaves me with one hand to pull up both bags. I'm wobbling.

"Mày là bạn tao," you are my friend. (Notice I used "*mày tao,*" reserved for good friends.)

"You understand me?"

"Not . . . really."

"You understand me right now?"

"Maybe."

She's yanking back the net. So predictable. *"Why did you not tell your friend?"*

"You . . . write . . . so . . . funny!!!"

Her shadow stares at me; angry lasers sear through me. She could push me with one finger and I'd topple into leech land. But I hear something build in her gut, gurgling up her chest into her throat, then out comes the longest laugh. She tilts her face toward the moon and I'm so relieved her cheeks are reaching for the sky. I laugh too.

I hold the net high and she gets her jar ready. Except the glowing lumps are gone.

"They are hiding. We were loud." She turns back to the bank. Yes!

My good friend is stubborn, stubborn, stubborn. She thinks if we stay quiet enough for long enough the glowing globs will return. So we're squatting on the bank, our bottoms inches above mud, like two gigantic, displaced frogs. Tiny needle pricks are crawling through my nearly dead legs. To think, I could be lounging on a mat right this minute and be ASLEEP! The things I do in the name of friendship.

I poke and repoke various parts of my legs double-checking for leeches, although Út whispered they don't live in city ponds. Another universal fact I'm supposed to know. My luck, the one leech in this pond would find me. I recheck for lumps again and again before allowing myself to believe I'm safe.

My body is half asleep, so after a while my brain is too, sinking into a night that belongs to the unseeables. They announce themselves, though, by screaming joys or sadnesses into the grayness at such a high decibel that all the noises coalesce into a soothing lull. If I weren't human, I'd probably never want to leave this place.

The air breathes out hot and muggy, as always, but after a while hot is just hot. It's true, a constant sticky film envelops my skin, but people have lived here for forever and they've managed to thrive. The world smells of mud and rot and nectar and grass . . . familiar. I can imagine maybe living here, not here in the pond, but somewhere near Út, not forever, but maybe for a summer. Vietnam might be home too.

"They won't come out," says a boy's voice near us. We jump and knock over the jars. Út holds up the net as a weapon.

Another boy calls out, *"Don't worry, we're not stupid enough to bother a foreigner. The police treat them like crisp money."*

A girl, *"Don't be scared. We can catch them for you."*

Figures walk out of the shadows. We are taller than they are. It's dark, but surely they're kids, grade school even.

Út admonishes them, *"Why aren't you sleeping?"*

The second boy laughs. *"This girl is funny."*

Why is Út funny, exactly? But I stay quiet.

The girl again, *"Five each. How many do you want?"*

"One each," Út counters. My friend is bargaining with street kids over the equivalent of a few cents.

Second boy, *"Ten frogs for forty."*

I squeeze Út's arm to make her say yes. It works. We get to stay on land while the kids wade all the way to the reeds and shake them and make noises. The glowing lumps hop out and the net goes down. So the trick is to shoo the frogs from their hiding spots. Who knew?

Just then we hear mopeds screeching to a stop. Van jumps down and screams, *"Do not touch my clients."*

Frogs and kids disappear.

Will this froggish night never end? I'm pretty sure capturing them is illegal, but no one is asking me. I saw on PBS you can't relocate things. Look what the Burmese pythons are doing to the Florida Everglades. But didn't Út say the village pond used to have glowing frogs? It was hard to listen to her soliloquy while on leech alert.

Út has words with spit for Van, who finally calls into the darkness for the kids to come out. But before they can round up more frogs, they have to fish for the sunken net. Before they can fish for the sunken net, they have to renegotiate their price. Annoying but admirable. Finally, ten frogs sit in ten jars, lids on. A glow illuminates from the jars like captured moonbeams. Hey, that's something Bà would say and I thought of it all by myself. When Út puts her face close, the glow reveals the soft gaze and melty grin of true love.

Út pays the kids right before we jump on the revved Hondas, which broke all kinds of park laws by riding near the pond. Van complained until I slipped him a fifty. Right before we take off, I jump off my ride and run over to the kids, pretending to thank them but slipping each twenty dollars, as in the bill that might get me followed. Dad would want me to take the risk.

CHAPTER 27

In the morning, Anh Minh belongs to us again. With him in charge, we can yawn and relax and be brainless. He has bargained for Van and LuLu to take us around, plus a Honda for himself to ride. He has a list of tourist attractions, numbered in order of cultural significance. As for masks, he has bought us our own, so we can return Chị QH's. She doesn't want them back.

After breakfast, we go to Hồ Hoàn Kiếm or Lake of the Restored Sword, a national treasure. It looks totally different in daylight, a tourist trap full of flags and souvenirs. Út and I play well our starring roles as gushing, first-time visitors. Anh Minh blabs on and on about the legend of a turtle swimming to the surface with a sword that a Vietnamese king used to beat the Chinese. The turtle is immortalized in a stone statue in the middle of the pond, complete with a sword in its mouth. No one can go near the statue or even the water. Oops.

Why does every story in Vietnam's four-thousand-year history involve a fight against some intruder? The Mongolians, the Chinese, the Japanese, the French, the Americans. Anh Minh is telling me why but I'm very sleepy.

Next, we visit a pagoda that sits on a tree trunk. Really cool actually. Then we zip through the French Quarter, where houses look like mansions, not stacked rectangles. I think I like the stacked rectangles better—they're very Vietnamese.

We stop to snack every hour, which tremendously helps Út and me stay awake. Anh Minh thinks of everything, always picking a stand where we could eat sitting on the Hondas. That way no one has to be the moped watcher.

We eat grilled squid as big as my chest and as tender as . . . a rope. It stinks like dried fish and you have to chew, chew, chew, but it's so good dipped in a hot, tangy, sweet sauce. We stop for *chè ba màu*, a dessert that even Montana is addicted to. It's sold in every corner in Little Saigon. Sugar, fresh coconut milk, tapioca strings, three kinds of beans. Don't go by the description, just try it.

The best is when we stop for corkscrew, pinkie-sized snails. This time, we pay the vendor's son to watch the Hondas because eating snails requires sitting down with full concentration. The snails come out steamed in a basket. You hold a snail in one hand, a sewing pin in the other. With skill, you use the pin to pull out the meat without breakage. If done right you get a string of curly meat, which is dipped in red-hot, garlicky, diluted fish sauce and brought to your mouth without dripping one drop. The stuff stinks more than the squids and if spilled it will take the kind of vigorous scrubbing that might remove your skin.

Van is an expert, taught by his big sis, Chị BêBê. He presents Anh Minh with a perfect piece of curly meat because he's in awe of the boy who won the scholarship where he was ranked thirty-sixth.

"I was only second and would not have gotten it if Út's sister had not declined," Anh Minh says.

"Why would anyone be dumb enough to refuse an experience overseas?"

"Every new school year she must sit in the back for weeks before slowly advancing to the front row. But she remembers everything she reads and hears. If that's dumb, I wish I were."

"I apologize. I'm so envious of everyone. Poor kids whose smarts extend to the clouds. Rich kids who get tutors and come out ahead. They receive tutoring from the same teachers who give out the tests," insists Van.

"The teachers tutor because their salaries aren't enough to survive. Consider the children who never get to enter the competition because their parents cannot afford kindergarten."

I feel so grown-up listening to them, although I'm sad. Why can't everyone go to kindergarten? It makes me feel like I don't know much. What else do I not know?

"Is everyone so driven?" I ask Anh Minh. "Where are the lazy, slacker kids?"

He laughs. "That's the privilege of those whose parents have achieved the top ranks. For the rest of us, we're all reaching for security, status, satisfaction. The same goals parents everywhere want for their children, only here the children want it even more for themselves."

A cell rings. It's Van's, who relays that his sister heard from Chị Quỳnh Huyền who heard from Cô Nga the dentist who heard from her sister Cô Hạnh that we must return immediately to the dentist's home. Bà is arriving in one hour and this evening we fly to the South. For a second I'm disappointed and wonder if Bà would go without me. Anh Minh's list of attractions does extend to two pages. Guilt, though, strikes me hard. I remember the reason for this trip and stand up.

I'm in front of the dentist's house, picking yet another armful of mosquito-proof grass. It's a weed, a grow-anywhere, in-any-dirt weed. Of course, I harassed Út about her holdout. *"You didn't ask,"* she said, barely looking up from her precious froggy jars. Anh Minh said the grass makes him itch worse than any mosquito bite. "Concentrate on making your blood salty, miss." Oh, that's so easy to do.

The detective and guard arrive in *Honda Ôms*. How young and hip. I bow to both, then pull the detective to the back courtyard.

"No tell alley *Cô Nga."* I don't know the translation for *alley*.

The detective leans in, listens, then pretends he doesn't

understand. I repeat myself, pantomiming surprised faces and mopeds slipping on greasy dirt.

"Ah," goes the detective.

"Hurt many speak if." I fold my hands into a prayer, and say, "Pllleeeaaassseee."

The detective starts talking, always a bad sign, and I catch something about disobedient children and consequences. That's when I yell for Anh Minh.

Anh Minh informs the detective that if he tells Cô Nga, then Cô Nga will fire Chị QH, then Chị QH will never write a letter for Chị BêBê, who won't be able to help Van with his dreams of studying overseas. Back and forth they go. The result: the detective insists it's his duty to report our stupidity. Ugh!

"Miss, you must provide him with somethin' he yearns for, otherwise what is your bargainin' power?"

"What does he want?"

"The question is what do you have?"

Five captured frogs (I can claim half, right?), inadequate capri pants, dried food bought weeks ago, a matching set of glowing-charcoal mask and hat, a suitcase full of grass—then I remember what else is stuffed in the suitcase. His powdery notebook.

The detective jumps higher than I thought possible.

"At once I must reclaim it to my possession."

Not so fast. Translation: he will get it back at the airport when Bà, Dad, and I board for LAX, provided he clears all obstacles so Bà can get her wish. And of course he must keep my and Út's adventure in the alley to himself. Deal?

The detective tries to intimidate me with glaring eyes buried in deep sockets and protected by twisty, salted-caterpillar eyebrows. I stare right back even though the young are not supposed to stare at the old. But this is an emergency.

"Children today! What will become of society?"

I don't blink. Actually, I do because I'm human, but I don't blink a lot. The detective finally sighs, not having anything to counterbargain with.

Then I remember Dad is supposed to be meeting us here. Anh Minh translates and the detective shakes his head. *"A case so urgent that he must meet us in Sài Gòn."*

It figures. I'm so going to complain and complain when I see him. Bà is his mother, Ông is his father, hello, can he not make some time for them? I, on the other hand, have been solid from day one. When home, I'm going to bring this up every chance I get.

Anh Minh says he must go pack because he and Út are going back to the village in the same van that should be bringing Bà soon. I'm sad to see him go, so I ask if he's ever been to Saigon, maybe he'd like to go with us. I know better than to ask Miss Busy with Frogs in Jars.

"No, miss, I have not the time. Too much preparation before school. And I cannot allow you to go south without knowin' that it is Sài Gòn, two words, both downward tones, not Saigon, and to be truly updated, the city has been renamed Thành phố Hồ Chí Minh since the war ended. Never write Hochiminh City, it is so many ways wrong. And it is Việt Nam, two words, the first a deep and glottal tone, not Vietnam. Historically . . ."

This is what I get for being considerate? Who can tell the difference except a true Vietnamese? Why be so picky? But I can't reason with him because he's going on and on about what foreigners did to his beloved language. Yawn.

We hear a van out front. I leave Anh Minh talking to the wind and run to Bà. I hug her and she hugs me back. As always, I sink into Tiger Balm and BenGay and soft, cool silk. How insane to think I could miss being with her when she finally reads Ông's message. It's her turn.

CHAPTER 28

Bà and I are stuck in a tiny, noisy hotel room. I thought Dad was obsessed with saving money, but the detective outfrugals (a word?) him by far. He and the guard wouldn't even stay here with us, saying it's too fancy. They're rooming somewhere else.

Bà and the guard talked forever yesterday, so quiet and private that even though I spied I couldn't hear a thing. I finally gave up and went to pack for Saigon, I mean Sài Gòn, taking care to switch the detective's notebook to Bà's bag just in case he's sly enough to search mine. I know he would never touch Bà's private belongings . . . simply not done.

When they dropped us off at this hotel late last night, the detective admonished us to stay put until he returns.

"Đi bao lâu?" I asked how long he would be gone. Let's move it,

this is my last obstacle, then home home home.

"Không biết." Of course the detective didn't know, then he launched into a long agonizing explanation. By then I had found a fascinating crack on the ceiling.

Whatever the detective and guard are doing it's got to be better than sitting in a tiny room without a TV or even a real fan. When I turned ours above level 2, the whole thing shut down.

As for Dad, surprise, he's not here. Here's Mom on the detective's phone: "Don't worry, he will be there. The little boy had to have surgery again and is not recovering well. But Dad will meet you there."

It's pointless to complain to Mom about Dad. They are a halo-ish couple doing halo-ish work and they always stick together. Bà, of course, understands her son's dilemma, saying, *"If he cannot arrive, it's already more than enough that you are here."* I think speaking in Vietnamese makes her unreasonably diplomatic. I might as well try to speak more of it.

Bà napped while I ordered room service for breakfast and lunch. Both times the waiter brought baguettes and triangles of cow cheese. I don't know if that was what they thought I ordered or if that was all they had. My Vietnamese is much better live, where people can see my expressions and gestures. I've started eating the fluffy beef jerky and dried banana sheets that have been jammed inside my backpack for weeks. Food is food.

I'm so bored, the kind where you bite off all your nails and wish they'd grow back instantly so you could bite them again.

I could try pronouncing each word in the book Út gave me. She pressed it into my hand before I climbed into the van for the airport. Didn't say anything, just ran off. What kind of a good-bye is that? I wasn't going to hug her, honest. I'm thinking of asking Mom and Dad to buy her a ticket to Laguna next summer. They do owe me. Montana will be out of her mind offering makeover tips, and Út will swat her off. I can't wait.

Út chose a book completely in Vietnamese. Like a preschooler, I did a picture read. It stars a frog, of course. Bà said in this folktale a frog goes to heaven to ask for rain during a long drought. I will have to learn to read Vietnamese. It can't be that hard. Every little kid here has learned it.

"Mấy giờ rồi con?" Bà is awake, asking for the time. Finally.

It's late afternoon. Out the window the world has reinvigorated after nap time. Oh no, SAT alert. Have I succeeded in abolishing them or did I not notice using them? Who cares, they're embedded inside me. Accept them.

"Bà đói quá." Bà says she's hungry. Score! That means she would never settle for a stale baguette and last-forever, nonrefrigerated cheese. She never eats dairy, saying it puts bubbles in her stomach. That's her delicate way of alluding to farts. I love the word fart, which has art in it. Who doesn't like art? Do you see how bored I am?

We are preparing to leave the hotel. I'm beyond the beyond

excited, as I've played every possible mind game in this room. Every crack already imagined as an animal, every ceiling stain a face. One has averted eyes and a shy smile, so HIM. Bà puts on her traveling suit, meaning she plans on staying out for a while. Happiness!

As soon as we step outside we go right back in. The air is ten times hotter than up north. Okay, I'm going to stop exaggerating. Five times hotter.

"We must ask for damp cloths or the heat of Sài Gòn will drain us in half an hour."

She sits in the lobby while I talk/pantomime at the front desk. It's literally one wooden desk with one man behind it. He also played waiter when I called for room service. He understands exactly what I want but refuses to hand over the cloths because the detective berated him into keeping us in the hotel/jail. Everyone fears Bà and I will get run over or mugged or lost. I have to call Bà over.

"Why should I fear my own city? I once knew the name of every flowering tree and the date each would open its petals to greet spring."

"The gentleman was adamant that you both must not leave our protection."

Bà holds out her gentle, grandmotherly hand, and the man has no choice but to reach into the square, single-person refrigerator behind him and pull out two folded cloths, wet, cold, and smelling of orange peels. Mom thought she was being green by composting citrus peels. I'm going to teach her to never buy air or fabric freshener again.

We step back outside, the cloths pressed tight against our napes. Shockingly better, like carrying around personalized air conditioners. We walk, holding hands along a wobbly sidewalk where we have to maneuver for space at each step. Our feet touch food baskets and stools and blankets holding endless things for sale. Most of all, we step around people, sitting or squatting or standing five deep. Noises ring out like millions of frogs. I must be missing a certain someone. As for the smells, I must be acclimating because everything has mingled into this scent called life.

Bà points across the street. A sign on a pole between two baskets says BÁNH CANH. That's her favorite food, the only time Mom and Dad could get her to leave the house.

But the vendor sits all the way across the street. Swarms of beeping mopeds zigzag past us in both directions. I didn't think it was possible, but traffic here makes Hà Nội look like a country town.

We step off the sidewalk, take two steps, get back on. Our cloths are getting warm. The man at the hotel desk must have been watching because he's right here, saying he'll get the soup for us.

Bà shakes her head. *"One cannot eat* bánh canh *cold, and the noodles must never sit in the broth."*

No doubt he has a grandmother and knows better than to argue. He takes Bà by the arm. I hang on to her blouse tail.

"The trick calls for not looking at any driver but listening to the engines," he says.

We step into the death zone, pause for two mopeds, step forward, pause for four mopeds, step forward, pause, step, pause, step, and we're across with limbs attached. I didn't do much, but I'm impressed with myself. The man jots back across like he's doing the cha-cha-cha, pausing and stepping in a joyful rhythm.

Most customers are squatting, holding bowls and chopsticks to their mouths, and sucking in thick, white noodles. Someone offers Bà a plastic chair, the kind you'd see in preschool. All over Vietnam, skinny and agile people sit on miniature chairs. Bà is lucky to get one. As I said, this is the land to be old in. Knees to her chin, Bà calls for two bowls. I can squat and eat with the best of them.

The seller sees us and nods. She rinses two bowls in a pot of grimy, dark water, dries them with an equally grimy towel, then by some miracle she pulls out a bacterial wipe, the kind that kills everything on contact. She skips this last step for the locals. Fine by me.

Her two baskets contain the entire *bánh canh* operation. One has the broth pot, kept hot somehow, with containers of noodles and veggies arranged on the lid. The other basket holds the rinse water, bowls, chopsticks. When the seller is ready to leave this spot, she'll put her stool on the pot lid, then carry away the baskets already attached to standing handles. The baskets swing on a pole balanced on her shoulder, one basket in front, one in back. How many times have I seen this image? Of course she's wearing soft, black pants and a cone hat. It's so Vietnam, I mean, Việt Nam!

After two bowls each, we're really thirsty. All we want is water, but none can be bought. Merchants around us do sell every kind of soda, but never diet ones because as far as I can tell no one is on a diet.

"Why would you pay for water when you can boil it at home?" one vendor asks while trying to sell us warm, carbonated orange drinks. So not the same.

We wander to a fruit stand and buy longans because I've always loved them. After peeling the hard brown shell, they look like eyeballs and after eating you get to spit out black-pupil seeds. Sugary and sticky, the fruit makes me even thirstier. But it's worth it.

"Let's get drinks from our hotel, get new cloths, and go visiting," Bà suggests. I don't know whom we're visiting but, of course, yes.

Problem: the hotel stands way on the other side.

We hold hands, step off the sidewalk. Mopeds roar past us like gigantic dragonflies. We step back on. I can hear Bà inhaling deeply. Then she holds up one palm to the traffic. Forward. Traffic weaves around us, pausing, speeding, swerving, beeping. Bà doesn't glance at any driver, keeps marching. No moped can go that fast, but I swear some come within hairlines of us. I expect to be hit any moment. Please, please, please, let my head remain undented. I couldn't stand it so I look at the drivers. They dodge us, slowing, braking, almost bored they're so used to maneuvering like guppies in an overcrowded tank. One looks like it's aiming right for us. I close my eyes. Suddenly, we're across!

Bà smiles like I've never seen before, long teeth flashing, cheekbones lifted high. If she can cross the street in Saigon, I mean, Sài Gòn, which seems twenty times more congested than Hà Nội, all right, five times, what else can she do?

***

The detective is waiting in the lobby, marching back and forth, one familiar, leathery finger waving at the front deskman. Seeing us, he has a new aim for that finger.

"Why have you risked going out? What if you were injured? We have not come this far to have our plans ruined by a moped collision."

He really is upset because I can understand every word. Bà just smiles and asks for water, which someone in the hotel has boiled and stored in glass bottles. We drink and drink and buy more.

"You must register the importance of remaining within this locale and be prepared to leave the instant I require your presence." Oh no, his vocabulary is resurging.

Bà sits down, eyes closing as she asks, *"Have you seen the letter?"*

The detective gives the most impatient sigh. *"The guard in spite of my insistence has not divulged the exact nature of your husband's message. I am conducting a monumental project based on faith. We are asking for permission to access the tunnels where your husband was held, a task that is proving as difficult as stopping a typhoon with my bare hands. Allow me to assure you I have many workers in place trying to dissolve the obstacles before us, and I sincerely hope I can call for your presence in a few days."*

"If you are not ready for us, why are you here?"

Why isn't he ready for us? I have a life, and I've been way patient, doesn't he know that?

"It is with utmost respect and regret that I must ask for . . ."

Bà stops him, asks him to turn around, fumbles with the pouch at her waist. A white envelope. How many did Dad give her?

"Again, I apologize, but the costs have reached beyond our predictions."

"What are you doing?"

"I assure you, it's best to remain knowledgeless."

"If you are hinting that you must bribe every official connected to the project, so be it. Tell them I am here for a final truth."

"Despite the consumption of time I assure you until my last breath I shall see this task to its completion."

His words are melodramatic but they work for him, they really do. I only have to understand half of them to get the message. He looks like he's far from done talking, but Bà bows and says she has much to see.

"With respect, I insist that you stay. . . ."

"Certainly, we both understand that at my age this trip represents my last look at the city that occupies my memories. Every person possesses a city that is truly her own. Sài Gòn is mine and I shall bow farewell before I cannot. My best and worst years interweaved into a life here. I'm certain you understand."

After that, even the detective gets a bit misty eyed. I'm going to learn to use words like Bà so I can persuade people without having to pout.

"How do you plan to move about?" asks the detective. Every time he's flustered, his words simplify.

I offer, *"Honda Ôm."*

Everyone looks at me like, how do I know about that? The detective knows, but he's a good actor. We agree a *Honda Ôm* would make Bà dizzy. A cab? Dizzier. A bus? Dizziest.

"Xe xích lô," the desk man offers. Bà and the detective nod immediately. I'm too embarrassed to admit I don't know what one is.

The detective has left, after giving endless advice about how to prevent this and that. But we are ready, with two bottles of boiled water, new cold cloths, and my pouch full of *đồng*s. Wait until Bà sees me bargain.

The deskman has gone to get our ride, which parks in front of fancy hotels because only tourists use them. I thought tourists take cabs, but what do I know? We wait in the lobby.

"Shall we visit Chùa Vĩnh Nghiêm? Your father always loved going there."

"Vâng." That's an extra respectful "yes, ma'am." She could take me to Vietnamese school and I'd be excited to go. Anything to not sit in that tiny room and watch life pass by right outside my window.

The deskman comes in to get us. Outside sits a shiny, glowing cyclo, complete with a red padded seat and yellow fringes around a red canopy already pulled down to block the late afternoon sun. The only bad part is the skinny, I mean skinny skinny, driver who has to pedal. Bà says not to worry, he's used to going uphill with a two-hundred-pound slaughtered pig.

This is how Bà bargains: she hands the driver a twenty-dollar bill. Simple, effective, not a wasted word.

CHAPTER 29

Forget *Honda Ôm*, *xe xích lô* is how to conquer Saigon, I mean, Sài Gòn, I mean Thành phố Hồ Chí Minh. Blah, Anh Minh has messed me up.

I ask Bà what she calls this city.

"My mind will always know it as Sài Gòn."

That's what I'll call it too. Now we settle in for a shady, breezy ride. With every bump we sink a little more into the thick padding. And I get to eat more longans, my favorite fruit, grown in California too. I love my life. I'm not hot, really full, cocooned from the traffic and noises and smells, and best of all, I'm with Bà.

"Ông and I ventured to Chùa Vĩnh Nghiêm only once together when your father was a newborn. The pagoda was just built, the most extravagant in all of Sài Gòn. Ông had to drive two round-trips on

the moped to bring everyone. You should have seen the way children were piled onto mopeds back then. Father driving, mother sitting with legs to one side behind him, a baby on her lap, the next two youngest squeezed between the parents, and two more sat on the gas tank in front of the father, protected by his arms outstretched to the steering wheel. But even if we tried such an arrangement, we would still need to pack on more.

"While I waited for Ông's return, I was unable to smooth my brows, thinking what if he doesn't show. But he did, meeting us by the ice-cream vendor. While I worried, the children who came with me loved the outing, and the more my brows remained twisted the more ice cream they ate.

"Any pagoda at Tết chocked of people and the incense smoke burned gray into your eyes. Still, we held on to our children and waited in the serpentine line to the statue of Ông Thần Đồng. He was huge, with glaring eyes and a snarling mouth carved from an ebony stone that jutted out of a wall and frightened the children to quietness. Legend said his heart, though, had the power to heal. When our turn came, I reached up as high as I could and touched the statue's lower foot. I rubbed it and brought his blessing to the face of each child. Seven rubs in all. Ông always looked away, not believing in superstition, but he held each of our children up to me without a word escaping from his lips.

"Fate did not grant him the privilege to see our children reach adulthood or the pleasure to witness our wrinkles writing stories on our faces, but in the time we were allowed, we knew our treasures."

***

We arrive at the temple. No one else seems to be here. The driver says he will wait for us. He is all sinew, from his neck to his arms to his calves. Dad bikes to and from work and I thought he is in shape, but nothing like this man. I don't feel guilty about him pedaling us anymore. He doesn't even look tired.

Bà presses another twenty-dollar bill into his callous palm.

He shakes his head. *"Your previous payment covers anywhere you'd like to go for the day."*

"Accept this for all those times when you did not receive your due."

The pagoda stands ornate and huge, with two sets of grand stairs leading to the main building, and off to one side sits a tower with layers of curly roofs. I count seven stories. Bà has seven children. I'm about to ask if seven has significance when Bà walks toward a stone statue. Towering above us is a snarling monster-man bouncing out of the wall.

Bà looks up at memories I can't see so I know to keep quiet. From somewhere comes a faint scent of jasmine incense. It's as quiet here as the streets are noisy. Somehow, they both equal my Vietnam.

After a while, Bà takes my hand and we walk toward the statue. She reaches as high as she can but she can't touch the lowest toe. It's true, you do shrink as you get older. So I hoist her up by her waist and we get there. She rubs the foot. I set her down. She rubs my face. I feel weirdly blessed.

CHAPTER 30

The next morning, we get up at six. Bà has a list of places she wants to visit and overnight she seems to have gained energy. I've never seen her brush her teeth or get dressed so fast. I, however, am still exhausted, but I get up, like the dutiful granddaughter that I am.

I keep wearing the same outfit bought with Chị QH in Hà Nội. Washed at night and hung up in the bathroom, it's guaranteed to be dry by morning. I don't know anyone here to care what I wear, much less how often and what brand. It's freeing.

We went everywhere yesterday, to national ancestral sites where I found out incense smoke can turn you blind temporarily, to a still-standing French restaurant that was Ông Bà's favorite, and she ordered a rabbit ragù that they always shared (I had chicken), to a park with a gigantic stone turtle, to a stone slide, to a dessert shop where Ông Bà took the children who ranked first in class. I told her today she would have to take all her children no matter their ranking or they will grow up and have low self-esteem. She looked at me like my imagination is too vivid.

Bà now stands. *"Let us eat breakfast, then shop for presents."*

My eyes seem to be glued together from the inside, opening them is such work. But I, outstanding child of the West, still drag myself after her.

Our *xích lô* driver is waiting out front. Again he refuses a twenty-dollar bill.

"Use it to buy treats for the children."

I have no idea if he will, but it does give him a way to accept without embarrassment. I like that.

After eating, I feel more alert. We stop at a bookstore. Bà looks at books on tape. It's perfect, her eyes are failing and where else can she find recordings in Vietnamese? She says she'll look for books on tape for me too. Great.

I wander into a section of books in English. Even better, bilingual books. I'm going to learn to read Vietnamese. Best yet, each book has a price tag. No bargaining needed. Thank you! I see a huge blue book called *Vietnam: A Natural History.* Look how they spelled it. This is my understanding: if a brain is thinking in English, it's Vietnam; if thinking in Vietnamese, Việt Nam. If you learned it as Việt Nam first, then your brain will think Việt Nam no matter the language. Unless you learned it as Vietnam and then become superfluent in Vietnamese, then your brain will switch to Việt Nam. Unless you learned it as Việt Nam but forgot your first language altogether, then your brain will think Vietnam. Why do I care?

Vietnam: A Natural History has a whole section on frogs, with illustrations. Út will flip. She already reads photocopies of scientific froggy journals in English, looking up just about every word. I could try doing that to read the froggy folktale. An English-Vietnamese dictionary does sit on my bookshelf. But maybe I can PDF the pages to Anh Minh as a translation project. He'd love it.

Next, the driver takes us to a building with a roof that covers a gigantic open market separated into hundreds of tiny cubicles, each a store. Even with no walls, it's humid, hot, and wild.

"How can people breathe?" I ask Bà.

She shrugs. *"They have been doing so for years."*

It turns out Bà shopped here way back when and knows exactly which corner of the market specializes in what. Not much has changed. One section has rows and rows of fabric. Every merchant selling the same things. Another section has souvenirs, another tea, another silverware, and on and on.

Bà buys ebony chopsticks embedded with iridescent seashells, handing the merchant ten dollars and not wanting change. She says she doesn't like carrying so much paper. Bargaining up at every stand, she becomes very popular.

Following her lead, I hand over dollar bills for sunshades that will fit over Anh Minh's John Lennon glasses. That way he won't have to squint. Then I see a whole row of sun-blocking masks, literally hundreds of them. I buy ten in skin colors and will anonymously get them to Cô Hạnh. They might inspire a relook at her own design.

Next to the masks are long gloves in every color. I've seen them on just about every female driver, wearing fancy party gloves up her elbows while zipping around in the sun. I buy red for me, so I can complete my look of a burning charcoal, now with jazz hands. Mom will want to borrow the whole outfit for gardening. I buy a yellow pair for Út. I can just see her face. She'll probably use them to capture tadpoles. And I buy ten pairs in all colors for Cô Hạnh. I'm sure she'll try to market her own version.

Suddenly, something like firecrackers explodes on the roof. It's the thickest rain ever. Every merchant with goods spread out in the sun scrambles to drag them under the roof. I actually see drops of rain big as kidney beans. Oops, an exaggeration. Big as corn kernels and they pop when they hit the pavement.

"Come out." Bà drags me.

I do what Bà wants because she's usually so sensible. I find myself in the rain with my face turned to the sky. Thousands of arrows slash down and prick at my face, longing to stab deeper and get at the muscles underneath. Oooowwww! I come out of shock and start pulling Bà back under the roof. Maybe the stress of waiting for the letter and for Dad has finally driven her senseless.

"Stand still, you will adjust," Bà says, keeping her face tilted upward.

Again, I listen. I can't leave her alone out in the biggest storm of the season, which is what people nearby are screaming. It helps to keep my head even, so the arrows land on top of my head, not painful but soft, like thousands of kisses. Bà isn't going in anyway. She's smiling.

"When I was little, how I waited for a strong summer rain. Such true pleasure. Each drop warm and soft as silk. Rain should always be warm, hot even. Legends say the droplets cleanse your mind the way ocean water heals your wounds."

Bà holds out both hands to form a cup; her face tilts up even more. The more her cup fills, the gentler her smile. I've never imagined her really young, a plump, happy little girl who rainbathed, probably naked like the children around us are doing right now. If only I could be so carefree. I'm fretting about how she might get a cold, how Dad would yell at me if and when he shows up, how she needs to stay healthy to see Ông's writing, how I have to get her back to the hotel and keep her dry. Caretaking is exhausting, I tell you, exhausting.

Finally, all kinds of people, done rescuing their goods, run up with umbrellas for Bà. I take one and cover her. She knocks it away.

The driver appears with his own umbrella and gently turns Bà toward his cyclo. She resists. They whisper. He takes down his umbrella and she agrees to walk. At the cyclo, he rolls up the shade so we can sit fully exposed to the rain. In this manner, with Bà cupping out both hands and opening her mouth to catch memories, we ride away.

I barely slept last night, my bones aching and my head throbbing. Bà, though, snored and snored. Besides, I kept waiting for her to sneeze, checking her forehead for a temperature. I'm now too tired to yawn but I still rock as her caretaker, asking if her throat is sore.

"My entire body has weakened, my child, but as long as I can stand, I shall visit this city."

Is that a cryptic way to say she's sick? Dad really should be here; he's the doctor. Where is he? He's so going to pay for making me worry like this.

I want to sleep but Bà has yet another list of places to visit and say bye. It's touching but what's wrong with waking up at ten instead of six? We're in no hurry. The detective keeps leaving messages that he's still sorting out arrangements and not ready for us. More waiting, I should be quite good at the waiting game by now. But I'm not. Waiting sucks.

Day one in Sài Gòn was kinda fun, seeing Bà eat rabbit and thinking of Ông. Day two was okay, although shopping among congested cubicles just about did me in. Then day three, back to the same temple with the bulging stone monster because Bà can't seem to say bye. Day four, yesterday, I dragged myself behind Bà and wondered why my bones hurt.

At one point, Bà left me in the cyclo because I whined too much. She went into yet another temple to offer incense. Sitting there, in the cyclo shade, in the middle of the afternoon, minding my own business, I got six whopping mosquito bites. Anyone who insists that mosquitoes only hunt from dusk till dawn needs to sit near me.

The bites swelled to the size of fat dimes. I had nothing to battle the mosquitoes with: the magical leaves were useless once dry so I had thrown them out, my one city outfit exposed my ankles, and neck and face, and despite eating gobs of salty pork, salty eggs, salty shrimps, pickled greens (not kidding), I still am too sugary.

Not only did the bites swell, they itched, bad. So I had no choice. I had to gather my own spit on the tip of my index finger and massage each pink mound. I rubbed and rubbed while thinking of Mom. She's actually all right sometimes. If I had my phone I would text: Spit zaps itch. She'd be so proud. The more I rubbed, the less I itched. The pink dots flattened and blended into my skin. I blew a kiss toward Mom in Laguna.

Now, the morning of day five, I shuffle after Bà to the lobby. No doubt the cyclo driver is waiting outside, stretched and ready for more nostalgic fun.

"I would like to inform you a phone message has been left in your name," the front-desk man tells Bà, the same thing he says every

morning. I think it's fine to be less formal, but he obviously enjoys his words. Another one.

Bà holds the receiver while the man punches keys to access the message. So retro, it's cool. Bà listens and breaks into a smile.

I don't believe it: today is the day. The detective will pick us up at 7:00 a.m. That's in twenty-seven minutes. My cheeks swell upward. The last hurdle, I tell myself, the last hurdle.

While waiting, we eat a breakfast made, yet again, of sticky rice and mung beans. It's really good, don't think I'm complaining. I'm just amazed how many kinds of treats can be made from two simple ingredients. Like all the things made from wheat and sugar back home. So maybe not that amazing.

Bà chose food that should keep us full for a long time, not knowing what to expect for the day. We are dressed in our sturdiest clothes, the only clothes we've worn. Bà in her traveling suit; me in my local outfit. I'm so done with washing by night, wearing by day. I shall burn this outfit upon landing in Laguna.

At exactly 7:00 a.m., the detective walks in, beaming.

"Such fortune the last few days, the rain softened the earth and sped our goals considerably. I'm honored to report all obstacles have been pacified and we await your arrival."

"We?"

"It took a crew of dozens and a signature of a colonel to allow this visit, but I have every reason to believe our hardship will prove

its worth. Let us go while the day is cool."

I ask, *"Wait for Dad?"*

The detective shakes his head. *"I regret to report I do not know his current status."*

CHAPTER 31

It's tense and quiet in the van. Everyone was hoping Dad would make it back, despite Bà's claims of understanding.

"Have you seen the letter?" Bà asks.

"No one has. The officials understand that you want to witness where your husband was held, but they have not been informed of a possible letter. It's best not to show our true purpose when any reason can be used to deny us. I have admonished the guard for not thinking ahead and removing whatever is in the tunnel, thus avoiding this exhausting excursion. But that man simply nodded. I do not know any more than what I've told you."

I can tell he's insulted the guard has not confided in him. The more upset he gets, the clearer his words. It's mean to wish the detective would remain upset, but that's what I'm wishing.

We inch forward and stop, inch forward and stop. The bigger the vehicle the more you're disadvantaged in this traffic. Compared to Hà Nội, Sài Gòn has more of everything. More drivers, more pedestrians, more shops, more noises, more telephone lines, more police, more stoplights, more girls in the tight, short cocktail dresses. Actually, no one dressed like this up north. The few who do here really pop out. Are they wearing thongs? They all wear masks and elbow gloves, of course, then it's all about exposed legs and arms. I notice Bà tries to not look at them. In Laguna, she had warned Mom to pack baggy pants for me, as not to show the shape of my butt, something no girl in her day would ever do. Now her old world has Las Vegas influences.

The same architect who designed up north must have come south because stacked rectangular houses rule here too. The bottom levels are used as shops. We just passed one house that somehow inserted rows of houseplants between the brick layers on the sides of the house, creating long, airy windows. It looks like it might even be cool inside. Maybe with a ceiling fan and a glass of lemonade, I could see myself living there.

We ride long enough for me and the detective to fall asleep. It's obvious he didn't sleep much last night either. We wake when the van stops. From the alarm in Bà's eyes, she recognizes this area.

"Here is Củ Chị?"

"I agree this region stirs deep emotions, but he left his message nowhere else."

I hold Bà's hand. It's sweaty, a first. I've never seen Bà sweat. Her eyes scan a land green again with bushes and vines. I wonder what Bà is thinking, but her eyes seem so far away I don't dare speak. We step into mud from the recent rain, and Bà squeezes my hand.

"Ông đã đi trên đất này," Ông had touched this same earth, Bà says, adding that the ground would have been dusty and worn, but Ông was indeed here during a dry season all those years ago.

A man in uniform comes out and bows to Bà. She barely nods. I sense she has paused her mind and her heart, holding in emotions, until she understands enough to release them. I don't know what to think or feel either.

Right then, another van pulls up, honking so much I'm embarrassed. The door opens and . . . Dad. I run over, slipping on mud, all my resentment evaporating. We throw ourselves into the tightest hug ever.

"Mai Mai, I'm so sorry. I never meant for you to shoulder this much on your own." Dad looks at me, really looks at me, with such intense eyes that to release the overwhelming emotions, I laugh. He hugs me again. "It's all right, everything is okay."

I believe him. We don't have time for my hundreds of questions because the man in uniform is waiting for us. We join Bà and the detective and the guard, whom I'm just now noticing. I wave; he waves back. Bà and I, on each side of Dad, lean into him.

Dozens of boys and men, each holding a shovel, watch us, nodding as if in approval. The man in uniform steps up to Dad.

"I apologize for the primitive nature of our operation, but I only

received permission to widen the passage by twenty-five centimeters on each side, just enough to fit one pulley. We added two ventilating fans to aid in breathing. Otherwise, we have left this obscure part of the tunnels intact. This is not where our tours are conducted. I can report no one has been in this part since the war's end."

I'm sure when he said "tunnels," Bà flinched. I'm so anxious I feel sick.

He brings us to a round hole in the ground, barely big enough for one person. Yet fresh dirt surrounds the mouth, meaning it was even smaller before being enlarged for us.

Addressing Bà, he says, *"I shall crawl in first, then assist you down. Don't worry, it's not a deep hole. Once in, I ask you to sit on a plank with your head as low as possible. Another staffer will crawl behind you to push while I pull. Prepared?"*

Bà seems to be in a dream. I have to yank the tail of her blouse, hard.

"Con đi," am going, I say it firmly to convey it's not an option. Did she not realize he did not mention me?

Bà finally is alarmed. *"Cháu phải đi,"* she must go, meaning me.

The man scowls and calls the detective over. They negotiate with the detective's hands permanently held in a pleading gesture. It's not going well.

I raise my hand like in class. They stop talking.

"Con xin theo Bà của con để được gặp Ông." I don't know where the words came from, but I think I said please allow me to go with Bà so I can meet Ông. I don't look away from the uniformed man

like I'm supposed to but smile at him with the same sadness I've seen on Bà thousands of times.

The man blinks. He must have relatives who went missing during the war and I bet he's still wondering what happened to them.

"Speak to no one of this. Permission was granted for the wife, that was all."

I stand close to Bà before he can change his mind. Dad steps up behind me, while the detective squeezes in behind him. The guard comes running over to make the tail. Good for him! The officer throws up his hands and scrunches his face. Dad approaches him, and after a tense talk and an offering of a white envelope, the officer walks away.

The guard climbs down first. Then Dad, who supports Bà into the tunnel as the detective and I help her from above. I see her on a wooden plank just wide and long enough for her to sit and pull up her knees. The plank has wheels and a cushion and can be pulled by a rope. To be old in this country! They pull her into the tunnel, making room for me. I jump down and suck in a breath from the shock of the heat. I hear fans blowing, but it's still really really hot, smelling of mold and rot and the earth and a strange floral scent, just sprayed. Once down, I get on my hands and knees to fit through the crawl space. I've never been so grateful for pants that cover my knees. Maybe I won't throw them away, after all. The detective comes in after me.

We move up when Dad pulls and I push Bà's plank, its wheels

creaking and cracking in the semidarkness. I barely push because Dad is superstrong, pulling and crawling while following the guard holding a flashlight. A long and narrow passage stretches out ahead of us. I can hear sighs from the detective, holding his own flashlight.

The damp and lumpy earth has ragged roots that poke through the soil, puncturing my knees. I ignore the pain. A few extra inches have been newly scraped on each side and above me. How narrow was it before? I try to breathe evenly, sucking in hot air each time I push the plank forward. It's not a smooth ride. The wheels bump over jagged clay, but Bà does not utter a single sigh. Once, I placed a palm on Bà's back, but her breathing sped up at my touch so I yanked my hand back. Our breaths and the *crick-crack* of the wheels mingle in the echo of the tunnel. I wish I could see Bà's face or hold her hand. She must be thinking of Ông crawling through this same passage. I think she just sucked in a sad breath.

We crawl and the guard calls out, "One meter." I push, breathe, crawl. "Two meters." Push, breathe, crawl. A meter equals 3.28 feet. After what seems like a long long time, my palms ached and knees scraped, the guard announces, "One more meter." Eleven in all, thirty-six feet, over six times my height. I'm exhausted.

The guard jumps down into a bigger space where he can stand, then Dad, who helps Bà. I hand him her plank. I jump down, grateful to stretch my frame upward, fully. How do you live for years where the ordinary act of standing becomes a luxury? And yet an entire army did.

Bà stands between me and Dad, each of us cradling one of her arms to keep her strong. I reach up and touch the ceiling, clay, roots, twisting together into nature's cement. I yank free a clump of clay and press it into Bà's hand. Something Ông might have touched. Bà leans into me, a warm, welcome weight.

Inside the earth, the darkness is so dark it feels suffocating. I open my mouth to suck in stale, scorching air. Still, it's precious circulated air, something Ông did not have. I force myself to stop thinking about what Ông thought or did or said to pass the many many hours in the putrid darkness. It's too much.

The detective comes down the hole with his own flashlight.

"What message could possibly have survived here?" Dad asks.

The guard answers by gliding his light along the dirt wall closest to us, then to a corner, keeps going, another corner, a wall, a corner, back to us. We're in a square.

"What is your light seeking?" Bà asks.

"It's here. I saw it when we tested the passageway and I alone reached this storage chamber."

The guard swivels his light faster and higher along the walls. The detective's light follows his.

"Ah, here," they both say.

Both lights now shine directly on the wall farthest from us. Marks have been scraped into the wall, leaving ragged holes. Bà sees something and stands taller.

The guard directs, *"Come at it from an angle. We need shadows to read it."*

Both lights now beam from the right, illuminating the holes to be alphabet letters scraped into the dirt by a shaky hand. A lot of letters. Each one stands on its own and for a second I think it's a code to be read only by Bà. But the more I stare the more obviously the letters are grouped together with upper cases and those tiny marks: *aưM tạH gnừT . . .*

"No, shine from the left to the right."

The two beams glide along the wall in unison and point from the opposite angle.

I hear Bà suck in a breath.

She mumbles as she follows the beams of light, *"Mong Nhớ Em Đếm Từng Hạt Mưa."*

I hear a wondrous "ah" as she reaches out a hand in the near darkness toward the writing.

I try not to breathe too hard, wishing that myself and the others could disappear so Bà can reread her letter in private. Read from the left, no one can mistake the familiar line Ông had written in every letter home, the line that came alive each time he called their children's names, the line that ached with longing for his wife as he counted his last years, months, weeks, and days.

Bà walks toward the words with Dad and me supporting her on each side. One light shows us where to step, the other illuminates our destination. Bà first, then I, then Dad, reach up and combine our hands and retrace each letter, imagining Ông scraping each line into the earth. It must have taken a long, long time, each letter and tiny mark chiseled into the rocklike clay with a stump of wood and a piece of metal.

While I stand there, nothing else matters, not the heat, the air, or the stench rising above a floral spray. Nothing matters as long as I can hear Bà's breathing elongate into full, satisfied breaths.

The crawl back doesn't seem half as long. Once out, I want to hug the natural air. Clean, fresh, and real. Bà thanks the detective and guard with words I don't understand and hands them each a white envelope. When they resist, she points to her heart.

Next, she and Dad approach the dozens of hired laborers nearby and hand twenty dollars to each. She bows, and every laborer returns the gesture.

The guard waits for us at the van. Before I can tell him thank you, Bà takes him aside for private words. It's pointless to spy because the detective can see me and he has no problems yelling at nosy children. He looks lighter, taller, the way I feel when I finish a long, difficult science project.

The guard walks away. His thin frame recedes from me and suddenly I see his wrinkly face twist back with a slight smile, aimed at me. We wave our final farewell.

An exhausted Dad falls asleep on the ride back. He looks like he hasn't been taking care of himself, cheeks sunken in, hair matted to his forehead. I'll have to help him clean up before Mom sees him.

During the long ride, Bà stares straight ahead. I know better than to disturb her. But once Bà reaches for my hand and pats it.

"Mãn nguyện, mãn nguyện."

I've never heard her use such words but from the serene look in her eyes she has been waiting to say these two words for a long long time.

CHAPTER 32

After one night of rest, I realize we could fly home right now. We're done. Dad doesn't say much but waits for Bà and me to decide. Bà doesn't say much but waits for me. Finally, all the planets and stars have aligned so that I get to name my ticket.

Dad even hands me his laptop to check for return flights. There are lots of flights to LAX, any time we're ready we can go. I'm ready! While on the internet, I email Mom the longest, drippiest letter. I know she's going to print it out and keep it. I write her even though Dad has told her everything. I write because I want to.

Then I can't help it, I click open my FB page. Yep, more butt bows and more Montana and HIM. But my heart doesn't jump. It could be the distance but I can't seem to get worked up about a triangle that, like so many other triangles, will eventually solve itself and life goes on.

I have friend requests. I click and can't believe it, one is from HIM, weeks ago. OMG, I've been here for thirty-one days. That's like a record. Of course, I confirm HIS request. I also have messages. I click and can't believe it, one is from HIM: "C U whn U get bk, Kevin."

I take back every mature, philosophical thought I just had about triangles. I'm still so interested in mine. Wow, a message from Kevin. His name in print. Whoever thought to put those five letters together in that order is a genius.

I'm about to read out the flight options.

And yet.

Bà has not let go of the clump of clay from the tunnel. It has stained her hand red, flaking into tiny bits. She doesn't say, but I see a wish in her eyes.

"Bà muốn gì," I ask her what she wants.

She takes a long time to think, debating whether to tell me.

I ask her to tell me.

"I would like to bring Ông to a final peace in his village, where his ancestors can watch over him as he drifts toward his next life. He has been unable to part from us as I have in selfishness been claiming him. Given a proper resting place, he will be able to bid farewell and resume the journeys of his being."

Dad is about to translate, but I stop him.

"I can listen, Dad."

I don't think Dad has ever looked at me deeper, longer, or gentler. "I can wait. Let's do this for Ông Bà."

Back in the village, we hold the ceremony the next day in the cool dawn hour. Just the three of us at the family plot. Bà chooses a spot in between Ông's parents, and Dad digs a small hole. In it Bà places a knotted handkerchief holding the clump of clay and a piece of blue tile. Not much, but enough.

Dad covers the hole, pouring a little water into the dry earth to pat it down.

Neither Bà nor Dad say anything because really, what is there to say?

We each light an incense stick. With their red tips glowing, the incense releases swirls to aid Bà in her chant. A low, throaty chant that lasts just long enough. We each bow three times before pushing the woody ends of our sticks into the damp spot. They all hold.

Bà stands still for a little while longer, then turns to go, with me and Dad on each side escorting her home.

Bà goes back to bed after breakfast. I don't think she's tired but likes lying in the room with the blue goddess, from which she has packed a few tiles to take home.

Out back, Dad slams me with the news. "I still have fourteen patients who have waited a year and they are simple cases. I'll wait and make my originally planned return flight. You go home with Bà. Call Mom. She'll arrange it."

I stand there waiting to get mad, but I can't. Why shouldn't he stay and follow through with his promise? For some reason I ask, "Does Bà want to go now?"

"We can't have you fly home alone, so she'll go with you."

With my family the answer is never easy. I've got to pull out the pertinent information, like a tug of war. "Just say it, Bà would rather wait and fly home with you, wouldn't she?"

"You'll have to ask her."

"But she probably won't tell me, the way you and Mom won't tell me how you left here or what life was like as refugees or anything that's not perfect."

Dad sighs. I expect he'll get mad. But he reaches out and side hugs my shoulder. What has happened to all our tempers? Are we going to be one of those lovey-dovey families? He turns my face to his. "My flaw is in wanting to present a flawless world to my only child, but you're old enough to listen. When we flew out at the end of the war I knew I was lucky to be on an airplane. Millions of others did not have that. I looked out my airplane window and saw a boy not much older than I was dangling from a helicopter. I watched him hang, then drop into the sky. I've always felt guilty—why him and not me? I've never been able to answer that: why does one human being have too much and another human cling to life in desperation? I wanted to present a clear view of a good life to you, but I'm finding out that's impossible."

"What are you talking about?"

He laughs. "That life is easy and hard, beautiful and ugly."

"You get philosophical like this when you don't eat enough."

He hugs me some more. "Don't sit here listening to your old man. Go find Út, go play."

"I'm not a kid, Dad. I haven't played since Montana and I were in grade school."

"That Montana, don't worry, she'll find her way too."

"To where?"

"When she gets there, she'll know. Go on, go do your thing."

I have a weird dad, but at least now he's really nice to me. I saved him this summer, he's said so over and over. I rock, oh yeah.

He's already gone, left before Bà even got up from her early nap. Dad said if I want to know about Mom's life, I have to listen, not so much to what she says but to what she doesn't. Listen to her sighs, the wishes in her eyes, the truths she's hiding, even from herself. Okay, that's a bit much. I'll work on that later.

Now we're getting ready for a good-bye lunch at Cô Hạnh's. I will hand out presents, and email Mom to discuss travel plans. I don't know whether to leave or stay.

Right now, Bà and I are working on getting to Cô Hạnh's, my ninja gear fully on. It's slow going. Halfway there, Bà stops in the village center to rest on a bench under *cây đa*.

Bà hasn't been talking much, which is understandable. Years

and years of waiting finally ended with a clump of clay and pieces of blue tile. I hope that's enough.

We sit facing the tree, and Bà leans into me, bony and light. She reaches out and traces the tiny crevices in the bark. Her translucent finger glows against the dark trunk. She's smiling a slow, quiet smile.

"Ông có đây," she says, meaning Ông was here, had touched the same bark, years ago.

I reach out and trace the bark with her. Ông exists all over this village. I have a feeling Bà is not ready to say bye. She's not sad though, holding her quiet smile; her other hand holds a piece of blue tile.

"At first the weight of loss was thrust upon me so harshly I could only take a short breath, just enough to endure the next few seconds, only to find I must inhale again. Every person in turmoil thinks the boulder on her chest will never lift. Yet the same boulder awakens an equally strong urge to live. The wind and the rain will wear the boulder down to manageable rocks, and those rocks will dwindle to pebbles, which will become sand and will grind yet smaller until it becomes dust and enters the blood. Yet it's far from done. The cycle will recirculate, boulder to dust then dust to boulder. Sometimes taking years, other times in a matter of minutes. From the outside, there might be no trace of a wound but I still remember because the memories have become as necessary as blood.

"I tell you of loss, my child, so you will listen, slowly, and know that in life every emotion is fated to rear itself within your being. Don't

judge it proper or ugly. It's simply there and yours. When you should happen to cry, then cry, knowing that just as easily you will laugh again and cry again. Your feelings will enter the currents of your core and there they shall remain."

I nod even though I'm just as confused by her talk as I was by Dad's. Did they plan this? Why all this talk of life? Is there something different about me?

Just then, Út comes running up, lifting her ninja mask to say everyone is waiting for us. She takes one side and I take the other and we get Bà to where we all need to go.

Cô Hạnh has everything planned down to Bà's every bite and sip of tea. Wonderful, I can take a break from caretaking.

Not just Bà, Cô Hạnh has planned everyone else's minutes too. The older villagers eat at their own tables with chairs that have back support. The detective sits here, with his notebook that I've returned, reading to Bà. No doubt he can go on for days and days.

The middle-agers are drinking cognac mixed with 7UP. Even I know that's a very weird mix, but everyone seems to like it.

The young-adult tables get the most meat because they're growing. The boys are back from shrimp camp and they can eat. Cô Hạnh seats Anh Minh and Chị Lan together, and I hear them call each other "anh em," so their triangle has cemented down to a solid pair. Don't fear for Con Ngọc. Cô Hạnh has her sitting with a muscular man/boy and their story is about to be set too. She's wearing that fluffy pink skirt, and I hope something less surprising underneath. She would do very well in Laguna, BTW.

I wish Cô Hạnh would come to Laguna and arrange my life. No doubt, I would be going to spring dances, homecoming, and prom with Kevin. It feels okay to let his name escape now that he's messaged me. Maybe that means something, maybe I won't need Cô Hạnh after all.

Út and I are at a table with teens who would rather be elsewhere. Everyone eats quickly and off each goes. Út and I escape to the back porch.

I thought for sure I'd be spending the afternoon watching Froggy sleep, oh the joy. But to my surprise, Cô Hạnh has hooked up a mosquito net on the back porch and hung a double hammock inside. How cool is that? We get in and before we settle into the hammock I give Út the book I got for her, wrapped in a banana leaf because, I don't know, just because.

Út flips through the pages, looking at each illustration. She is so slow. Finally, she gets to the section on North Vietnam and to the chapter on paa frogs (Genus *Paa*). She breaks into a huge smile and proceeds to read it in incomprehensible French-accented English.

I can't handle it and take over: "Species in the genus *Paa* go by a variety of common names in English, including paa frogs, spiny frogs, and mountain bullfrogs." Út listens enraptured. So we lie in the hammock with our heads in opposite directions and I read the rest of the chapter.

"Very good," Út says. Let it register that she has complimented me, out loud, in English. Who knew such a thing was possible?

"Do . . . you . . . understand?"

"No, *but I listen.*"

"I could . . . teach . . . you . . . to . . . pronounce," I say before thinking.

"Yes, now."

What have I gotten myself into?

She doesn't know yet, that Bà and I might be leaving in a day or two. But Út should have guessed because we're at a good-bye party, hello. Út is Út, so she probably didn't care to find out. What if I stayed another twelve days and flew home with Dad? He'd love it because he wouldn't have to pay three hundred dollars, or four bicycles, to alter the return date for me and Bà. Four of Dad's patients would be getting new bicycles. That's something.

"Teach me," Út says. *"I will be taking an examination to qualify to study with a scientist who lives deep in the jungle to collect data on frogs. I have to say the scientific names in English."*

I read another chapter to test my level of interest. Could I really spend twelve days reading about frogs and salamanders and newts? Út would love it. Bà too would love to have more time to spend with the tangible objects Ông had touched. I have a feeling she would be visiting his little spot in the family plot and watering the mound holding the clump of clay and the chip of blue tile.

Maybe I can stay and maybe I would enjoy it. What's in Laguna that's so urgent? Mom is exhausted with her trial and I will see Kevin when I see him. As for Montana, I can wait.

Út shakes the book in my hand. "Read."

"Why? . . . You . . . don't . . . understand."

"That's why I must listen."

"Identification of all paa frogs remains challenging because the spines are both seasonal and restricted to mature males (though some adult female Yunnan paa frogs also have spines on their fingers). Complicating matters, the current taxonomy . . ."

I look up and Út has her eyes half closed, dreaming. She's going to want me to pronounce every word in this dense, thick book. Maybe I can't do this.

"Keep reading, *why have you stopped?*"

"I . . . can't . . . stay . . . all . . . summer."

"Everybody knows. Twelve more days, twelve more good-bye parties."

"For . . . real?" I have to admit, I'm flattered. Cô Hạnh has planned twelve parties for us. I wonder what we're eating next.

"Read."

Can I deal with bossy Út in two languages for twelve days?

"If I . . . read . . . what . . . do . . . I get?"

Út sits up, rocking the balance of the hammock. I'm sure she's searching high and low for something to counterbargain with. I mean, I'm reading a textbook about frogs and other slimy stuff, what does she have?

"You name *one of my glowing frogs.*"

Hmm, Út just spoke in half English, half Vietnamese and her offer is not bad.

"*Mày có*, what else?" I too can speak half and half. Notice how I used "mày" for good friends.

"I let you open quả sung *and feed my frog.*"

Hmm, that is intriguing. I could video the episode and entertain Mom. Her case is not going any better.

"What else?"

Út looks at me, twisty browed, then lies back down to think. I lie back too. Each of us has a leg off the hammock, and when one pushes, the other lifts her leg, then vice versa. A rhythm happens, push, rest, push, rest, and soon Út starts talking in Vietnamese to herself about how it's her dream, like dream dream, to go into the jungle and study frogs. I have to admit it's soothing and sweet just lying here listening. The hammock keeps swinging, Út keeps talking, and soon half asleep, I start talking in English about the first time I heard Kevin speak.

"We were discussing this poem that ended with the line, 'Nobody, not even the rain, has such small hands,' and Kevin out of nowhere said maybe he loved her so much that—"

Út interrupts, "e.e. cummings."

I shoot up and stare at her. "*Mày* know?"

"Good poem. *We heard a recording of it over and over in class.*"

How can she possibly have memorized a poem I just read last year, with help in English class?

"If I . . . pronounce . . . every . . . word . . . in the entire . . . book, *mày có* teach . . . me to read . . . in Vietnamese?"

Út knits her brows, no doubt plotting the precise steps for my language acquisition. She stares hard, perhaps assessing my brain's potential, then announces, "Eel." I know she means "deal."

Right then, I decide to stay.

ACKNOWLEDGMENTS

To Tara Weikum, who knows all editing things,

to Rosemary Stimola, who knows all things in general,

to Janine and Caden Robinson for Laguna Beach tidbits,

to Amy Wilson, Chris Schmidt, Jonna White, Suzanne Weeks, Lori Ganz, Kara McCormick-Lyons, and Diggy Moneypenny Cockerham, who kept my daughter busy during deadlines,

to Brianna Lai for letting me ask too many questions,

to my An, who inspired this novel,

to my mother, whose sentences really do land in drops of bells, and of course, to my Henri, who makes a writing life, and thus life, possible,

thank you.

AUTHOR'S NOTE

Hello readers,

Thank you for reading *Listen, Slowly*. I had so much fun getting inside Mai/Mia's head that it wasn't work at all.

I also want to thank the readers who have contributed to my charity, Viet Kids Inc., which buys bicycles for poor students in the countryside of Viet Nam. Every week or so, I get a surprise in my email account, notifying me that a random reader has found his or her way to Viet Kids. Now I love checking my emails.

I started this charity back in 2005 when I traveled to a coastal city in Viet Nam as a translator for a group of doctors doing cleft palate and burn surgeries (like the father character in *Listen, Slowly*). Between surgeries I chitchatted with patients ages eight to sixteen and asked what they wanted most. I thought they would say this or that toy or something electronic or some dish they wanted to eat. But 99 percent wanted a bicycle.

With a bike—not a fancy hybrid or dirt, just a plain three-speeder—each student can zip to school in twenty minutes or so, instead of walking an hour or more each way. Often, a rider would take along a sibling. Without a bike, by the time students get to school, they are usually too exhausted to learn.

Outside of school, the bike is useful for the whole family, as a parent can take vegetables to sell at the market or go to a clinic without walking half a day.

A bicycle still is the easiest and fastest solution to an easier life for Vietnamese living in the countryside. An aside . . . when I asked students in the cities what they wanted most, each said a moped. I replied, "Get a job."

I came home and immediately started Viet Kids Inc. Find out more at thanhhalai.com.

Thank you and keep reading,

Thanhhà

VIETNAMESE GLOSSARY & PRONUNCIATION GUIDE

áo dài (ow zai): a type of traditional Vietnamese women's clothing

Bà (bah): grandmother

Bắc (bahk): a title given to a man older than your father, but younger than your grandfather

cảm ơn (cahm uhn): Thank you.

cao quá đi (cow kwah dee): So tall.

chào (chow [falling tone]): Hello.

cháo (chow [rising tone]): hot rice porridge

Chị (chee): older sister

chờ đây (chuh day): Wait here.

Chờ được không? (chuh duhk kohng): Can you wait?

Cho gì? (chaw zee): For what?

Cô (koh): aunt

Cờ đến tay, phải phất. (kuh den tai, fai fat): Flag in hand, must wave it.

còn đau (con [falling tone] dow): Still hurts.

Con khổ (con koh): I'm suffering.

Con qua ngày mai. (con kwah ngai mai): I will come tomorrow.

dau quá (dow kwah): Such pain.

Đây (day): here

Đến rồi (den roh-ee): We're already here.

Đi ăn rồi đi bộ? (dee ahn roh-ee dee boh): Go eat, then go walk?

Đi rồi. (dee roh-ee): He's gone.

đồng (dohng): Vietnamese money unit

đúng (doong): yes

gương (goo-ung): mirror

Hà Nội (hah noh-ee): Hanoi, the capital of Vietnam

Honda Ôm (honda ohm): type of Honda moped

không (kohng): no; not

không biết (kohng bee-it): I don't know.

không chịu được (kohng chee-oo duhk): Can't bear it.

không có đau (kohng caw dow): Not in pain.

không sạch (kohng saik): not clean

không sao đâu (kohng sow doh): Do not worry.

làm (lahm): make

Làm gì? (lahm zee): What to do?

Làm sao? (lahm sow): How?

mặt trái xoan (maht try swan): pretty, oval face

mày (mai): you

Máy giờ rồi con? (may zuh roh-ee con): What time is it?

Mày là bạn tao (mai lah bahn tao): You are my friend.

mày tao (mai tao): good friend; literally "you me"

Mong Nhớ Em Đếm Từng Hạt Mưa (mong nyuh am dem tuhng haht moo-uh): Longing Missing You Counting Each Drop of Rain; each word is the name of each of Ông Bà's children

Muốn về (moo-uhn veh): want home

Nam Mô A Di Đà Phật, Nam Mô Quan Thế Âm Bồ Tát (nahm moh ah zee dah fuht, nahm moh kwahn teh ahm boh taht): a Buddhist chant

Ông (ohng): grandfather

Ông Bà (ohng bah): grandfather and grandmother; usually referred to as one entity

Ông sống? (ohng sohng): Ông alive?

phải giúp (fai zoop): Must help.

phở (fuh): a Vietnamese noodle soup

rau muống (rao moo-ung): a plant used in cooking

Sài Gòn (sai gon): Saigon

tao (tao): me

Tết (tet): New Year's celebration

tìm người canh Ông (teem ng-oo-uh-ee kah-ing ohng): find person guard Ông

tuổi dậy-thì (too-uh-ee day tee): age of puberty, fifteen or sixteen

Việt Nam (vee-it nahm): Vietnam

Xanh (sahn): blue

xe xích lô (seh sic low): Vietnamese cyclo

Xin lỗi. (seen loh-ee): I'm sorry.

Turn the page for a special look at Thanhhà Lại's

Inside Out & Back Again,

A NEWBERY HONOR BOOK and
NATIONAL BOOK AWARD WINNER.

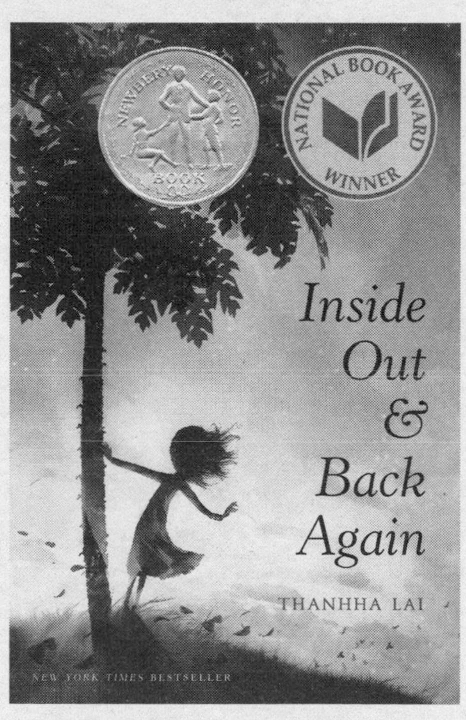

1975: Year of the Cat

Today is Tết,
the first day
of the lunar calendar.

Every Tết
we eat sugary lotus seeds
and glutinous rice cakes.
We wear all new clothes,
even underneath.

Mother warns
how we act today
foretells the whole year.

Everyone must smile
no matter how we feel.

No one can sweep,
for why sweep away hope?
No one can splash water,
for why splash away joy?

Today
we all gain one year in age,
no matter the date we were born.
Tết, our New Year's,
doubles as everyone's birthday.

Now I am ten, learning
to embroider circular stitches,
to calculate fractions into percentages,
to nurse my papaya tree to bear many fruits.

But last night I pouted
when Mother insisted
one of my brothers
must rise first
this morning
to bless our house
because only male feet
can bring luck.

An old, angry knot
expanded in my throat.

I decided
to wake before dawn
and tap my big toe

to the tile floor
first.

Not even Mother,
sleeping beside me, knew.

February 11
Tết

Inside Out

Every new year Mother visits
the I Ching Teller of Fate.
This year he predicts
our lives will twist inside out.

Maybe soldiers will no longer
patrol our neighborhood,
maybe I can jump rope
after dark,
maybe the whistles
that tell Mother
to push us under the bed
will stop screeching.

But I heard
on the playground
this year's *bánh chưng*,
eaten only during Tết,
will be smeared in blood.

The war is coming
closer to home.

February 12

Kim Hà

My name is Hà.

Brother Quang remembers
I was as red and fat
as a baby hippopotamus
when he first saw me,
inspiring the name
Hà Mã,
River Horse.

Brother Vũ screams, *Hà Ya*,
and makes me jump
every time
he breaks wood or bricks
in imitation of Bruce Lee.

Brother Khôi calls me
Mother's Tail
because I'm always
three steps from her.

I can't make my brothers
go live elsewhere,
but I can
hide their sandals.

We each have but one pair,
much needed
during this dry season
when the earth stings.

Mother tells me
to ignore my brothers.
We named you Kim Hà,
after the Golden (Kim) *River* (Hà),
where Father and I
once strolled in the evenings.

My parents had no idea
what three older brothers
can do
to the simple name
Hà.

Mother tells me,
They tease you
because they adore you.

She's wrong,
but I still love
being near her, even more than I love

my papaya tree.
I will offer her
its first fruit.

Every day

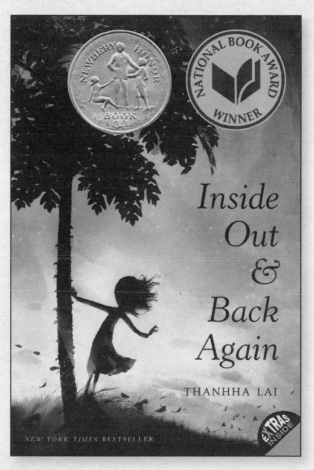